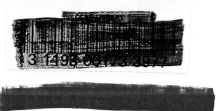

3 1495 001 /3 3977

Gunning for Ho : Vietnam
stories

AUG 04 2011

GUNNING FOR HO

D0036992

Western Literature Series

University of Nevada Press ▲▲ Reno & Las Vegas

H. Lee Barnes

GUNNING FOR HO

Vietnam Stories

Afterword by John Clark Pratt

Western Literature Series

University of Nevada Press, Reno,

Nevada 89557 USA

Manufactured in the United States of America

Design by Carrie Nelson House

Library of Congress Cataloging-in-

Publication Data

Barnes, H. Lee, 1944–

Gunning for Ho : Vietnam stories /

H. Lee Barnes ; afterword by John Clark Pratt.

p.   cm. — (Western literature series)

ISBN 0-87417-346-9 (pbk. : alk. paper)

1. Vietnamese Conflict, 1961–1975—Fiction.

2. Vietnamese Conflict, 1961–1975—United

States—Influence Fiction. I. Title. II. Series.

PS3552.A673854G86   2000   99-37249

813'.54—dc21 CIP

The paper used in this book meets the

requirements of American National Standard

for Information Sciences—Permanence of

Paper for Printed Library Materials, ANSI

Z39.48-1984. Binding materials were

selected for strength and durability.

09   08   07   06

5   4   3   2

Contents

Acknowledgments

Stories in *Gunning for Ho* first appeared, some in slightly different versions, in the following journals: "A Lovely Day in the A Shau Valley," *Clackamas Literary Review* 1 (1997); "Stonehands and the Tigress," *Clackamas Literary Review* 2, no. 1 (1998); "The Cat in the Cage," *Flint Hills Review* (1999); "A Return," *Lost Creek Letters* (Autumn 1991); "Plateau Lands," *Echoes* no. 17 (1997); "Tunnel Rat," *Clackamas Literary Review* 3, no. 1 (1999); "Gunning for Ho," *Flint Hills Review* (1999).

I wish to express appreciation to the editors who selected these stories for publication, and special thanks to Tim Schell, who nominated "A Lovely Day in the A Shau Valley" and "Stonehands and the Tigress" for the Pushcart Prize.

I am pleased to mention, in this first book, people who have assisted, guided, or otherwise supported my writing efforts or the publishing of this collection: Tonja Page, for insisting I could write when I couldn't; Joyce Standish, for her long-standing support and keen eye; Ron Carlson, friend and mentor, for his sage counsel and skilled readings; Alberto (Tito) Ríos, for his tough criticism and kind reassurance; Valerie Miner, for her sensibilities and many generous praises; Richard Wiley, for investing time and friendly advice; Trudy McMurrin, for seeing the vision in these stories; John Clark Pratt, for coming aboard and offering important suggestions; and Rich Logsdon, Chuck Adams, and Bob Dodge, for being superb teachers and loyal friends, and for thinking me much better at this writing game than I am.

I thank you for gifts given that I can never repay.

GUNNING FOR HO

A Lovely Day in the A Shau Valley

Marines at Marble Mountain claimed A Shau was filled with juju; MACV Intelligence said it was filled with a regiment of North Vietnamese. In either case, it was one bad place to go. The men of Delta Company, Fourth Battalion, knew a fierce battle had been waged there four years before and another two years after that. From time to time thereafter NVA had used it as a staging ground, for A Shau remained a primary infiltration route on the Ho Chi Minh Trail.

One at a time the helicopters angled northward, tilted their noses and began the descent. They followed an azimuth north by northwest so as to come out of the rising sun. Ahead on the port side Anderson could see the ghostlike shadows of the craft slipping across the lush green canopy. So, this was A Shau Valley. His wife would love to fly over this. She talked often about exotic lands, the Amazon and the Congo.

He glanced at Candy and Small. Small chewed gum and winked to mollify fear. Candy licked his teeth to do the same. Everyone had a ritual to calm his private dread. As he always did before hitting an LZ, Anderson chambered a round in his M-16 and pictured his wife oscillating beneath a parachute, waving and smiling at him, when they had been in Acapulco on their honeymoon. He framed the image of her in his mind and fixed it there. If it was time for him to die, he wanted to take that one moment with him. It was only fancy now, a fiction to relieve fear, but not then, not when she'd gone up, not once but three times.

Small chewed gum and winked again. Candy ran his tongue over his teeth and squirmed. Anderson clutched his M-16 and watched the ground rush by. As the Huey approached the LZ, it trembled, rotors flattening the tall grass, struts leveling just above ground. Small was out first. The rest of Fire Team Alpha quickly followed. Candy dropped to the ground and flipped the safety catch of his M-60.

The next chopper landed as the first lifted off, and another after that, and another. As each landed, the men flying out of the belly took possession of another small plot of ground. The LZ was cold, a good sign, and when the last of the choppers had landed its cargo of men, the pilots screwed their Hueys down the valley floor, gaining speed for the steep climb over the Annamese peaks.

The men of Delta Company formed two columns and headed west. They marched an hour before the captain brought them to a halt on a rocky crest that overlooked the deep recesses of the valley, a stretch of jungle marred with craters. The camp and airstrip were obtrusive landmarks. Here a pilot had won a Medal of Honor, as had the Green Beret captain who'd led a company of Chinese mercenaries into the camp to save the few Americans who'd survived the siege. Captain Salazar ordered up Fire Team Alpha to scout the camp.

Spec Four Phillips, the rifle leader, squatted beside Lieutenant Lamb and Captain Salazar, who pointed out land features leading to the camp. "Can you scout it in, say, an hour?" Phillips looked at the dense growth on the valley floor and replied, "Yes, sir, if no one trips a mine."

Fire Team Alpha moved out, Small taking point, Anderson behind him, followed by Candy with his M-60 and Rutkowski with the M-79 grenade launcher, then Phillips, T.P. with the radio, and Sensibar bringing up the rear. Small, Phillips, and T.P. were bloods, and Rutkowski and Sensibar were white, while Anderson was half Mexican and Candy was half Shoshone, but showed none of his father's white blood.

Field-hardened, conditioned like tennis players, they carried somewhere around sixty pounds of gear on their shoulders as they moved steadily but with great deliberation through the undergrowth. The dense forest swallowed the sounds of their footsteps but not the clatter of metal. Caution marked every movement. Each man watched where the man in front stepped, for there were land mines. Each was guarded by the one behind and protected by the one in front, as it was essential to survival that every man depend on every other man. They were grunts, armed beasts of burden, individuals and not individuals. Names and numbers, each with his own history, they faced the same uncertain future. They believed in luck and signs. They believed in each other when there was nothing else to believe in. And that's what made them men.

Sensibar was the professor, always reading. He was a natural killer. T.P., a great basketball guard in high school, had flunked out his freshman year at St. Joseph's because he never got around to attending class. T.P. and Sensibar were buddies. That's why Sensibar followed behind, keeping careful watch.

Phillips, who hailed from Arkansas, had apprenticed as a carpenter and wished only to go home to a girl named Louisa who'd promised to give him ten children. Candy was the quiet one, staying to himself. He seemed to most like Rutkowski, who was from Massachusetts and told stories about his father and uncles, who were cops. Candy wanted to be a cop. Rutkowski wanted to be a craps dealer on the Strip in Las Vegas and make fifty thousand a year. Candy was the newest man. T.P. had called him Chief the first day Candy arrived. Candy had asked if it was okay to call T.P. Nigger, which caused a moment of strained silence. T.P. shook his head. Other than his wanting to be a cop and not wanting to be called Chief, not much was known about Candy. He'd replaced Gable, who'd gone home without a scratch.

Small had large greenish-yellow eyes that showed in striking contrast to his caramel complexion. He planned to be a lawyer someday. He was uncanny at point. He had a beautiful wife who as a fashion model earned ten times his soldier's salary. Small and Anderson, the only draftees in the squad, were best friends. Anderson, called Chico by his squad mates, was the handsome one. He had dark wavy hair and white teeth that glistened when he smiled. His wife was a bank teller in Tucson who wrote him approximately the same letter twice a week.

They moved without resting and without speaking, taking cues from Small, who seemed to have 360-degree vision. The valley was still—no bird sounds, not even an occasional monkey screech—quiet and unnerving. At one point T.P. whispered to Sensibar that it was worse than spooky. Sensibar nodded and said he had the feeling they were being followed, but he could neither see nor hear anything.

Small was the first to spot the edge of the camp and called Phillips forward. On that perimeter four years before, a Green Beret sergeant had single-handedly held off two NVA companies, and North Vietnamese bodies had piled up so high that a pilot flying close air support had named it the Wall of Dead.

Now, four years later, the forest was reclaiming the land that the Americans had cut out of its tentacles. Where the earth was charred from nitrates, brush and vine and even a few stunted trees grew, some out of bunkers, some out of bomb craters. The barbed wire had long ago rusted.

Phillips called the rest of the squad forward and asked for two men to scout the camp. Sensibar, standing next to T.P., volunteered the two of them, but Phillips wanted T.P. on the radio. He called up Captain Salazar and told him they were going in and sent Anderson with Sensibar.

Tall grass and brush covered their approach to the edge of the camp, but there the ground had been so defoliated that only a few sickly looking stems grew and everything else was withered and brown. In the open now, they belly-crawled under the rusted wire. The damp red clay smelled of mildew and nitrates. The old bunkers, wood beams splintered and rotting, reeked of stale water.

Anderson viewed the devastation and shook his head, wondering if soldiers had been buried under the rubble. For an instant he swore he felt something brush his ear and cheek. Sensibar held his M-16 at his waist and turned from north to east to south to west. Everywhere they looked, they saw evidence of a great struggle that oddly seemed unfinished.

The two of them advanced, one moving as the other covered. They found craters and rot and vegetation asserting itself through the crust of red clay, and more rot and more destruction, a graphic record of events — a bunker where a young Green Beret took a direct hit from a rocket-propelled grenade; the Wall of Dead where, nourished by human blood, clumps of grass grew thick; another bunker where a commo man destroyed the coded pads and blew himself up before the enemy got to him. At that very spot, after the camp had been overrun, the North Vietnamese had gathered to celebrate. In the midst of their celebration a downpour of incendiaries and five-hundred-pounders had fallen out of the clouds.

A thousand North Vietnamese had died taking a strip of earth they couldn't hold. Sensibar and Anderson were like bats without sonar. Sensibar sank to his knees at the apex of the camp, took off his steel pot, and rubbed his forehead. Anderson squatted beside him. Sensibar shook his head. Anderson understood. They could comprehend bullets and shrapnel from mortars or grenades, but this ruin was not war as they knew it. Sensibar claimed he didn't believe in ghosts but said they should leave before he started to. What would they tell the others? Nothing there, was all they could report, so Anderson told Phillips the camp was creepy but clear of vc. Phillips radioed the captain.

The fire team formed a tight circle, facing outward. Phillips and Sensibar smoked. Sensibar's hands trembled. Anderson rested his head against the trunk of a tree and tried to picture his wife. He couldn't. The sun was overhead and crisp in a pastel-blue sky. The day, though hot, was not sweltering. Flies buzzed about, annoying the fire team as they waited in the shade for Delta Company.

An hour later the company arrived. They took ground by advancing one squad at a time until they occupied the camp and the edge of the airstrip. Like the members of Fire Team Alpha, the rest of the soldiers in the company appeared to be affected by the devastation. Told by the first sergeant to dig in, they kept an eye out for mines and booby traps. One man uncovered an arm bone, quickly buried it, and moved two steps away. Once fields of fire were laid out, the officers went about checking on their platoons.

Anderson, better now, was joking with Small about ghosts. Sensibar, however, couldn't stop the tremors in his hands. T.P. told him that if he stopped smoking his hands wouldn't shake, besides cigarettes could kill. Sensibar frowned, doused the cigarette, and looked beyond the shadows of the trees at the deserted camp. Anderson wondered why the company had come there. He asked Phillips's opinion.

"Chico, do I look like a general? We're here. 'At's all."

Okay, that's the life of a grunt, Anderson thought, and opened a can of peaches, drinking the syrup before spooning a peach. Rutkowski ate ham and lima beans. He chewed slowly as he watched a vagrant cloud drifting south. Speaking as much to himself as to his companions, he said, "A guy rolled fourteen straight passes at the Sahara in Vegas. Guy wins a measly eleven hundred bucks and someone else wins a quarter of a million. Guess luck's got everything to do with it if you got money in the first place."

Small asked Rutkowski what dessert came in his rations. Rutkowski opened the can and said, "Orcos, man. You can't have 'em."

Small shrugged and looked west toward the edge of the rain forest where eight men in khaki NVA uniforms stepped out of the shadows at the wood line, one waving a white flag. Small jumped to his feet and pointed as he shouted, "Charley's here!" The Americans aimed their weapons at the North Vietnamese. As the others stood their ground, one stepped forward and slowly advanced, his hands in the air.

Captain Salazar asked First Sergeant Tremble, a veteran of three tours, how his Vietnamese was.

The first sergeant shrugged. "Probably better than their English, sir, but not by much."

"You think they want to surrender?"

"Sir, I never seen nothin' like this."

They watched the lone man advance. Behind him the soldier with the white flag smiled and waved it back and forth with increasing vigor. Head erect and shoulders back, the Vietnamese lowered his hands and walked through a gap between two squads at the perimeter. A small man, even by Vietnamese standards, he offered himself as if much larger. His face was so flat it was almost two-dimensional. Judging from his carriage he was an officer, and probably a field grade. Each American he walked by turned to watch his passing. As he reached Captain Salazar, he looked back at the man waving the flag and motioned for him to stop. He saluted and held it until the captain returned the salute.

Salazar said, "Go to it, Top."

Tremble cleared his throat and said, "Ngày tuyệt vòi."

The officer grinned and gazed about at the soldiers manning positions nearby, then said to the first sergeant in a precise occidental accent, "It won't be necessary for you to stretch your linguistic skills, Sergeant. I am quite good at your tongue, and, yes, it is a lovely day, which I will expand upon shortly."

Captain Salazar, a tall, rangy man, pressed his tongue to his lips and looked down at the diminutive officer. "I'm Captain Salazar. Where'd you learn English?"

The officer lifted his open palms and shrugged. "I'm Colonel Tram Van Nim. I was educated at a boys' school in Singapore by an English staff and later took an engineering degree at the University of California, the one in Berkeley, of course. I understand my alma mater supports our claim to this country and indicts your presence here. I'm not surprised."

Captain Salazar, standing upright to emphasize his momentary position of superiority, pointed at the white flag. "Does that mean you want to surrender?"

The colonel merely smiled and raised his left hand. Immediately hundreds of soldiers in khaki uniforms flowed out of the shadows of the rain forest.

The captain nodded his appreciation. "You've got almost as many Communists as Berkeley," he said.

The colonel was unflappable. "Yes. The socialist revolution, Captain. You see we've not come to surrender."

"Are you asking us to surrender, then?"

Now the colonel smiled. "Your bourgeois country is not without its wonders. The hamburger. Wonderful, don't you agree? But I don't suppose you have any hamburgers? No. Actually, I've come to ask a favor."

"A favor?"

"Yes. May I . . . invite some of my men to join us?"

"Unarmed?"

"Of course."

Captain Salazar shrugged as if to say things were going well so far, why not? The colonel raised his hand and motioned toward the body of men behind him. A half dozen men in shorts and sneakers came to the front of the line. They carried with them three large canvas bags as they trotted through the camp. They stopped directly behind the colonel and dropped the bags.

"Please open them," the colonel said.

Sergeant Tremble stooped over, loosened the cord on one bag. "Baseball gloves," he said.

"A gift from the heavens," the colonel said. "Psy-Ops. Dropped by parachute by your Air America in Laos to convert the villagers to capitalism, a clever idea if only they knew what baseball is. We've carried this with us for over a year now, and I've instructed my men as best I can in the elementary facets. They practice as often as possible. This is a war, you know. But to the point. You see, along with hamburgers, baseball is the finest product of your decadent country. As the sergeant said, 'It is a lovely day,' and we wish to have a game."

Captain Salazar removed his steel helmet and rubbed the sweat off his balding head. "Let me get this straight. You want to play baseball . . . with us?"

"I think that is correct. Do you play the game?"

The captain looked at Tremble. "Do we play?"

"Sir, you can bet your sweet ass we do."

The colonel waved again to his charges, and a group dropped their rifles and headed to the airstrip. He smiled again at the captain. "We have a diamond camouflaged at the airstrip. It's crude but it serves its purpose."

Delta Company watched a hundred men sweep across the airstrip to clean away the blanket of shrubbery used to conceal the field. Some Americans had walked over that very area without noticing anything peculiar. The camouflage removed, they clearly saw the pitcher's mound and base paths, even foul lines in the outfield. The colonel had understated his assessment of the field. Saturated with scrub and rocks and cavities, the field was marred all the way to the woods about three hundred feet from home plate.

Leaving a shell of men to hold the camp, Delta Company marched to the airstrip. As every man but three had volunteered to compete, the captain, a fair man, decided it best to determine his team by holding batting practice.

"A lot of divots," he said to the colonel.

"Yes, we did the best we could. Many of my players injured themselves, but it's not so bad now that the mines seem to be gone."

"Mines?"

"Does that present a difficulty?"

The captain looked at the three hundred feet between home plate and the woods and smiled. It was a home-run park if he'd ever seen one. "No, sir. As you said, this is a war, and mines are a part of war."

"Yes, quite. My feelings exactly. I suppose we should use some officers as officials and swear them to honorable decisions."

When they shook hands, the colonel asked Captain Salazar the name of his team. Salazar grinned and squinted at the trees. "The Yankees. And yours?"

"The Giants, of course," the colonel said.

Captain Salazar thought to laugh, but the colonel wished him good fortune, then quickly went to join his men.

The Vietnamese positioned themselves on either side of the field and squatted to watch. They seemed amused as the Americans who took the infield picked up rocks from the base paths and tossed them off the field. But their amusement ended when they saw how well the Americans could sling a baseball around the infield. The air filled with the pop of the hardball on a leather glove.

T.P. had pitched for his school's baseball team. He took the mound as Anderson caught and promptly struck out the first four Americans. Then Candy hit a booming fly ball and was the first player selected. Sensibar, shaky hands and all, proved to be a fine power hitter. Small dinked a judy hit in the shallow outfield and had to earn his way into the lineup by showing off his fielding skills at shortstop. Rutkowski struck out and immediately started booking bets, making the Americans a five-run favorite.

When Anderson's turn came, he slammed a ball in the gap between shortstop and second and turned it into a double, but the highlight of practice came when Phillips cracked a line drive to left that climbed and climbed until it disappeared over the distant treetops, a boomer that brought the Vietnamese to their feet applauding and caused the Americans to cheer. Rutkowski changed the odds to get more action, making the Americans a nine-run favorite.

The North Vietnamese Giants, as home team, took the field in the top of the inning. After seeing the Americans hit, their pitcher was at first shaky but he settled down—not, however, until the Americans had scored two runs. A thin little man, he threw mostly junk, sinkers, sliders, knuckleballs, junk. The colonel had truly studied the game and taught his wards well.

With Anderson at the plate chatting and encouraging him with every pitch, T.P. put the North Vietnamese down in order. The colonel studied each and every motion T.P. used, each swing every batter took. Delta Company hit three homers in one inning, and Small stole second in the third inning and home in the fourth. The Americans asserted their superiority in every phase of the game. So it went until the fifth. The colonel put in a fresh pitcher and changed all but three members of his lineup.

T.P., who had only a fastball and an outside curve, suddenly faced batters who choked up on their bats and crowded the plate, taking the outside edge of the plate away from him. He walked two and grounded one out. The next batter up hit a fly ball to shallow left. The American covering left field charged in after the ball but fell into a hollow where he slammed to ground. The ball landed two feet away from him and rolled to a stop.

As the fielder was carried off with a broken ankle, T.P. gave the next batter a hard stare, but he wasn't the same pitcher he'd been for the first five innings. The Giants promptly recorded seven hits and five runs, a bad inning, but T.P. got out of it when one of the

Vietnamese hit into a double play, and the third baseman tagged out another who was standing off base scratching his head because he didn't catch the colonel's signal to steal home.

The sixth inning was no better for T.P. He let the first two batters on base with granny hits over the second baseman. Anderson and Tremble met on the mound.

"He's lost it," Anderson said.

"I can see it," Tremble said.

"Hey, guys, those jokers got lucky. Hell, they're midget-size. Got lucky."

Tremble leaned his face into T.P.'s. "Lucky? You call nine or ten hits in a row lucky? Y'er outta here," he said and sent T.P. to the outfield and brought in a kid named Schofield who threw three warm-ups and began firing bricks into Anderson's glove. What he lacked in placement, Schofield made up for in power. Still, the Vietnamese pushed two runners home. After that, the game settled into a defensive battle for two innings. In the seventh one of the Vietnamese dove after a ball in the outfield and planted his head in a hole. Another missed catching a rifle-shot drive at second with his glove but stopped it with his face. He lost three teeth. Candy made a save in the bottom of the seventh on a fly ball that was heading out, and at the end of eight the score was even at eleven.

In the top of the eighth Phillips took second on a sliding steal. The Vietnamese cheered him, and several of them ran up and down the sidelines throwing themselves to the ground and sliding, oblivious to the rocks they kept landing on. Thereafter, every Vietnamese who ran the bases dropped to the ground and slid in. One hit a home run and slid into every base he crossed, including home. The Americans shouted that wasn't the way the game was played, but the North Vietnamese spectators went wild over his performance.

In the top of the ninth Phillips hit a towering home run that landed out of sight in the trees. Sensibar stumbled on a rock and bruised his knee going to second on an easy double. Instead of tagging him out, the Vietnamese held up play until he was able to stand. Then as he limped about, changing direction, they put him out on a run-down play. The colonel cheered from the bench. The Americans were astonished—that also wasn't how the game was played.

After Delta Company scored three in the top of the ninth, the colonel, brushing off his hands, crossed the field and looked up at Captain Salazar. "It's a wonderful game, isn't it? I've been thinking. The one mistake Americans make is playing to win and not for the joy. Today we will play until we can play no more."

"But, Colonel, that's not how the game is played."

The colonel was unyielding. "I will not waste your time by speaking of baseball as a metaphor for life. You are surrounded by two thousand men and twenty mortars. The game is played the way I described. Now you must argue with the umpire over the decision."

"But the umpire is Lieutenant Lamb, and the decision was yours."

"I know, but I told my men of managers arguing with officials, so you and I will argue with the umpire."

They debated it at home plate, Captain Salazar kicking dirt as he hollered about the unfairness of the decision, and the colonel picking up a bat and throwing it down the right-field sideline. The spectators roared approval.

Play resumed. Anderson held the ball, ready to throw it to the mound, then something in it struck him. It had a face, not human features, but a face nonetheless, smudged eyes and cheeks, and an impish mouth turned up in a grin. He grinned back at the face, cranked his arm, and let the ball fly to the mound.

The players played through exhaustion and leg cramps and thirst and hunger, swung bats and threw balls and stole bases and applauded each other's plays and patted each other on the back and slapped hands and congratulated their opponents. By five o'clock the teams had lost track of the score, which was 27 to 19 or 29 to 17, for no one was sure, and sometime later they lost track of innings as well. More than twenty, they figured. When the injured were carried off the field, replacements ran out onto it, shouting and chattering. They played with the intensity of small boys, begging for one more hour of play, shouting at fielding errors, and applauding each hit or cheering a strikeout.

Time took on the character of a rubber band as each moment, each action, stretched into the next. Those who'd played from the start found renewed energy each time they took the field. As Small was about to step into the batter's box for the twelfth or thirteenth time—no one could be sure—Anderson told him they were just imagining this, that it was a collective fantasy concocted in their minds, a trip into ordered insanity. Small pounded a homer, driving in two runs. As he touched home plate, he shouted that there was nothing more real than the feel of the fat of a bat on the hide of a hardball.

Rutkowski, the only American left with enough arm to use as a pitcher, tossed the last daylight pitch, a ball. The sun sank over the crest of the Annamese peaks and formed a golden halo behind the purple tips of the mountains, but play didn't halt. The teams played on. It didn't matter that they couldn't see. No one wanted to quit, but that one inning took forty minutes without ending, and eventually they had to stop because they'd lost all the balls.

As the players stood and waited for one more ball to come out of the canvas sack, the colonel held the last bag upside down to signal that there were no more. He crossed the infield, shook the captain's hand, and told him it had been a lovely day. He complimented the skill and courage of the Yankees, and Captain Salazar expressed his amazement at the talent of the North Vietnamese Giants. The competitors embraced in the middle of the diamond. Captain Salazar suggested that in the morning the two forces go into the forest, find the balls, and resume play. The colonel stared at him blankly and said, "Captain, we must not forget our purpose for being here."

So the bodies of men withdrew from one another as shadows recede in the dark. Time that had taken on the character of a rubber band now took on the character of a spring, tense, capable of violent recoil, and the two bodies of men took on the tribal aspect of primitive rivals. Their world diminished, possibilities evaporated. When the Vietnamese returned to the rain forest, A Shau was again silent and filled with juju. The Americans dug in.

Later that night, after Tremble told him guards had spotted the North Vietnamese forming up at the airstrip, Captain Salazar called in a B-52 strike on all sides of the camp, but not before the mortars and machine-gun fire began. The North Vietnamese fired from the wood line surrounding the camp. Over the booming sounds of the incoming mortars, the first sergeant shouted orders — "Watch west for the first wave, kiddies! Charley's playing rough! Keep your heads down. Get some automatic fire on that airstrip." Anderson crouched down in his hole and tried to picture his wife, but it was hard when the ground around him was shaking from the impact of 120 mm mortars.

Finally the first of the bombs landed. The air raid lasted just twenty minutes. The force of the five-hundred-pounders made the ground shudder and spewed out orgasms of shimmering light that transmuted the forest into gypsy shadows. Soon afterward Puff the Magic Dragon passed over and stapled the jungle floor with a million grains of lead. The forest fell silent, except for the buzz of mosquitoes and the chirp of crickets. After that the Vietnamese came. The sappers came first, then the first wave of soldiers, and when those bodies piled up at the perimeter, a second wave followed. They gained nothing. A second bomb strike rained down on the woods. This lasted longer than the first, and the second silence took control of the night.

Anderson looked at the sky from his hole. As a field of black clouds slid past the round moon, all he could see behind the shadows was a shimmering hardball suspended beyond the reach of his hand. He'd not fired a round.

At dawn, as they looked out from their foxholes, the men

of Delta Company saw hundreds of trees snapped and tossed about like matchsticks and craters the size of watering holes and mounds of red clay charred and smoldering and they saw one another and they saw the sky blueing up overhead, but they saw no dead at the edge of the camp. The bodies that had ringed the camp had vanished. The men waited for another assault, but there was no sign of NVA anywhere. Slowly the Americans crawled out of their holes. Some ran hands up and down their limbs. Others sought silent company. A few opened up Cs and began eating. In the still air only the sounds of men breathing and can openers prying at tin lids could be heard.

They'd been lucky. The unit had taken two KIAS and three wounded, a miracle considering the intensity of the incoming. The captain called in dust offs for the casualties and told First Sergeant Tremble to have the company prepare to leave. At mid-afternoon a squadron of Hueys slipped over the eastern range and descended. As they boarded the craft, First Sergeant Tremble shook the hands of the men of Fire Team Alpha for playing so well.

When they were airborne and drifting away, Anderson happened to look back and down at the airstrip, now largely obliterated. Only the left sideline of the outfield was intact. He blinked several times to make certain he was seeing what he thought he saw—two men, mere dots, two-legged ant-men running up and back, throwing themselves down and sliding with near-perfect form.

Anderson nudged Small to get his attention, but Small, already smiling his usual smile, popped a stick of gum in his mouth, looked away and began chewing. Candy ran his tongue over his molars. Anderson leaned back, closed his eyes, and pictured his wife hanging beneath the white canopy of a parachute. She was smiling and waving, and he was holding a baseball up for her to see. It was glowing silver-white in his hand and had a face, a flat face with an impish grin.

Stonehands and the Tigress

Contending a monotonous mantle of vegetation — palms the width of a man's chest and trees the girth of mine shafts — Second Squad, Third Platoon marched single file up the bitter ascent. The climb had been most difficult the last hour. The combe was riddled with vine tangles and elephant grass, a habitat for spiders and mosquitoes and leeches, and for snakes — cobras and little green vipers called two-step death. Though aware of every swaying branch, every strange sound, every smell, every silence, the grunts, as they called themselves with ambivalent pride, moved with machinelike apathy, ants tirelessly lugging great burdens. A Shau was open to sudden mortar attacks and fierce ambushes, booby traps and tunnels and punji stakes.

They'd humped three hours now. Sweat blackened their fatigues and burned acidlike in the fine cuts left by blades of razor-sharp grass. Halverson halted them in a rocky clearing atop a ridge, where they tossed off their helmets and eased out of pack straps gravid with grenades and cartridge cases. Some dropped to the ground and sprawled out spraddle-legged on the spot. Some fired up cigarettes while others found shade or a tree to lean against. They wiped away sweat with green bandanas and sipped tepid water from canteens, water that barely slaked their thirst.

As he sipped, Stonehands gazed at the elongated depression below where miles of verdant treetops ran to a horizon of jagged peaks that blurred into a blue sky. He held his M-60 in the crook of his left arm. Two belts of ammo crossed his shoulders, one feeding into the machine gun, which he and the others called a pig. A tall man with long, powerful thighs, he was solid and flat in the chest, and wide and slightly stooped forward at the shoulders. His name was Walter Harvey, but he'd not been called that since jump school where he'd dropped two opponents in the first rounds of his only fights—two pickup matches.

Near Stonehands, Donatello sprinkled his trouser cuffs with insect repellent. A cigarette dangled from his lips. Roughly the height of an average Vietnamese, he was a wiry man who'd husband insect spray and batteries and recycle cigarette butts like a miser, then turn around and blow a month's pay on beer and boom-boom girls in Quang Ngai. He hailed from New York, a place, so far as Stonehands could tell, where the populace distrusted everyone but politicians.

Donatello said, "Should'a stayed at Benning," and pointed at Stonehands's M-60. "You'd be boxin'. Instead you're humpin' that pig."

Stonehands pretended to listen. His thoughts were aimed on a particular boy. He was stumped as to why after months of sweeping villages, of seeing bodies burned or riddled with holes, the boy in Hai Drong came to mind so often. Why not Howkert, who'd been found in a gutter in Quang Ngai City with strips of skin sliced from his chest?

As operations go, Hai Drong had been unremarkable—two sniper rounds, a captured vc turned over to the arvn. Only the boy made it different. He'd come straight up the middle of the road on a rough-hewn crutch smiling a gap-toothed smile like he was the local Welcome Wagon, his left arm gone, his left leg off at the knee. As he moved, his body listed to the right and he swung his good leg forward violently like a cricket hopping on one leg.

They'd fed him candy and canned peaches, given him cigarettes and watched him smoke. He'd called each of them Joe. They'd named him Sammy, a name he seemed to like. Someone crowned his head with a fatigue cap, and when it was time to go, he followed along as if one of them. *Di di mau*, he was told—no go with Joe. He'd struggled to keep up, hopping fiercely down the same road, following with the smile glued to his face as if that could change their minds. Then he fell and sat in the middle of the road and watched them leave.

"Be in fat city in Benning, Stoners. That colonel liked you."

Donatello spoke so loudly Stonehands had to look. He grunted. Boxing was behind him, a backslapping experience, curious and short-lived. After hearing of his matches, his mother insisted he see a chaplain and get a job "helping. No fighting." She hadn't raised her boy to hurt men with his fists. He'd explained that no such jobs existed, that the Army expected men to be violent.

"You're my son. Do as you're told," she'd said.

Stonehands was a good son. He'd not taken the colonel's offer and had quit boxing.

A few yards away Drammel stood, field-stripped his cigarette and unbuttoned his fly as he eased into the bush.

"Watch out a snake don't bite you," Donatello said.

Drammel shook off Donatello's comment and entered a vine tangle to urinate. He was a shy freckle-faced kid who twisted words when excited. Listed among his phobias were snakes, spiders, and elevators. He liked to say the one good thing about

Vietnam was no elevators. An instant later he came out, buttoning up as he charged through the bush. Aiming a finger in the direction he'd come from, he looked at Stonehands, then Halverson, and said, "A mockin' funky hole while pliffin' by the ease."

"He's talkin' in tongues again," Donatello said.

Halverson sat Drammel down and told him to take a few deep breaths.

Once he understood Drammel had found a hole, Halverson ordered the squad to set up a fire perimeter and said to Stonehands, "Bring that pig over here."

Stonehands stood at the mouth of the hole and kept his M-60 at the ready as Donatello removed a silver chain given to him by a boom-boom girl in Quang Ngai. A lucky tiger's claw dangled from it. He laid the necklace in Halverson's open palm along with a pack of cigarettes and took a flashlight from the sergeant's other hand, but not the .45. He knelt before the hole, flipped on the light, and peered in. He said it didn't seem to be a tunnel, too shallow, no more than six to seven feet deep. Halverson ordered him to check it out anyhow.

Donatello squirmed in and vanished. An instant later, he shouted, "Well, damn." At once, a tiger cub with rosettes on its back shot out, clawing at the ground. Donatello held a rear leg firmly in his grasp. He quickly stuffed the flashlight in his trousers and lifted the cub into the air by the nape of the neck, where it hung limply.

Stonehands shook his head. He'd grown up around bears and deer and owls, understood, as Donatello never could, the gravity of removing the cub. What did a kid from New York know?

"Put it back," Stonehands said.

Donatello smiled. "Looks harmless enough now, don't it, Hal?"

Halverson tickled the pink inside of its ear. The cub shook its head. "Cute, ain't it?" Halverson said. "I don't see no harm."

The cub seemed to like the attention. Halverson grinned as Donatello handed it over to him. Halverson scratched the tuft on its chin. Donatello hung the tiger's claw around his neck and reached for the animal.

"You bein' a fool, Donatello," Stonehands said. "Put it back 'fore its momma come."

Donatello licked his wrist where the cub had clawed him, then said, "Well, you just open her up with that pig, Bro." He took the cub from Halverson and tussled with it as he wrapped it up in his bandana. He smiled and stuffed it inside his shirt so that only its head stuck out. The cub closed its eyes as it licked sweat from Donatello's chest.

"See, Stoners, it likes me already."

"It don't know you yet."

Donatello laughed.

At the forward fire base Donatello scavenged three bags of powdered milk and a jar of honey and drained the syrup out of a can of fruit to feed the cub. Men came to the tent to see. It was a welcome break from the monotonous low drama of war and the petty annoyance of fear. It was a piece of home, a pet, something not yet ruined by the war. The captain stuck his head inside for a peek and reminded the men that a regiment of North Vietnamese was operating in the A Shau. He didn't mention the cub, which meant he wasn't going to cause a stir.

One man donated a poncho liner, another two cans of evaporated milk sent by an aunt from Milwaukee. Still another said the cub was a sign, good luck, and should be made the company mascot. Donatello said Drammel was the company mascot and dangled his claw necklace in front of the cub, which lay on its back swatting at it. When the visitors left, the squad lit a joint. As the weed passed from hand to hand, Donatello romped with the cub. He asked what to name it, and the squad began compiling a list, the favorite name being Butter.

McPherson, a sad-faced kid from First Squad, said the Montagnards believe a tiger has supernatural powers, that it is part animal, human, and spirit.

"What'a you know?" Donatello asked.

It sounded like a challenge, and McPherson, being timid, seemed apologetic when he explained he'd read it somewhere.

"Where?" Donatello demanded.

Jurgens, a spec four from another platoon, said, "I know somethin' about tigers."

Donatello said, "Let McPherson finish."

"I read about animal myths," McPherson said. He seemed to wait for Donatello to take issue, but Donatello was distracted by the cub, which had found its footing and was trying to run away.

McPherson swallowed and explained that according to the story the tiger had descended from kings and queens who ruled the forest before the coming of the Annamese and is driven to mate because its spirit can pass into the heaven of kings only if it leaves behind posterity.

"That's it?" Donatello said.

McPherson gave a nod.

Donatello said, "That's dumb."

Jurgens nodded knowingly. "Ain't either. Tigers," he said, "ain't other animals. Not here. Had me a shack-up in Quang Ngai who told about a princess."

Fists stuffed in his pockets, Stonehands stood to the side and listened as Jurgens told the legend of a princess who ran away with a lover, a Radai, a great hunter-warrior, rather than marry the Annamese king she was promised to. The couple was tracked down by the king's soldiers, and the Radai dismembered, his remains strewn over the highlands. Thereafter, Jurgens explained, the princess refused to eat, died, and was sent to the spirit world on a pyre, though he called it a "pier." According to his boom-boom girl, the tigress leaped out of the flames and killed the Annamese king. Always hungry, she had, he claimed, "roamed the jungle ever since in search of her lover's spirit."

Donatello gathered the cub in his arms. "Fairy tales are for kids. Besides, what does a pier have to do with tigers?"

"Uh, uh, he means a pu-pu-pyre," Drammel said.

"It's cute," Jurgens said, "but I wouldn't want to meet its momma, even if she is a goddamn princess."

The others were skeptical and joked about it, but Stonehands felt something resonant in these stories. Ain't right to mess with the natural, he thought, but a lot of things weren't right. Howkert, the boy, the vc. The image of the boy on the crutch came like a curtain, closing his mind to anything else.

Donatello stood up from playing with the cub. "Thinks I'm his mommy. Whachu think of the name?" he asked.

Stonehands blinked but didn't answer.

"Well, man, what about Butter?"

"You hear what those boys said?" Stonehands asked.

"You superstitious, Stonehands? 'S 'at what's buggin' you? You scared?"

Stonehands saw nothing wrong with fear or superstition. Luck and prudence, it seemed to him, had everything to do with everything.

"S-s-s-Stonehands a-ain't a-afraid of nuh-nuh-nothing," Drammel said.

"Didn't you hear, Bro?" Donatello said to Stonehands. "It's unlucky to be superstitious." He laughed and looked at the others. "Get it?" He clutched the cub to his chest.

Too fatigued to argue, Stonehands shook his head and lifted his tent flap. Outside he was met by Halverson, who told him he had last watch at a listening post. "You got four hours to get some shut-eye."

"After humpin' all day?" Stonehands said.

Halverson shrugged. "Sorry."

Three hours of blackness at a listening post! Stonehands shrugged and went to his own tent. He lay down and tried to think of something pleasant to whisk him into sleep, but there was the boy again, hand outstretched for candy, and the cub, swatting at the claw. These two fused into a picture of Howkert sitting next to Stonehands, saying he was through. Through? Stonehands hadn't understood at the time what Howkert had meant—crazy talk, rambling words about the only thing to live for and finding love and never seeing things the same. Stonehands closed his eyes and saw the narrow trail to his home in the Smokies, a turn in the path, and his house on the right, its windows open, a bluebottle fly buzzing by his head, and smells. . . . In the dream the boy came hopping down the road, but the road led to Stonehands's home. Then the boy was engulfed in a ball of darkness that swirled like a cyclone.

Tim Grofield, the sergeant of the guard, shook Stonehands's shoulder. "You awake, Harvey?"

Stonehands awoke and sat upright in the dark.

"Yeah, Sarge."

"You sure? You were talking in your sleep."

"I'm sure."

"Come on, then," the platoon sergeant said.

Stonehands slipped into his boots, tied the laces, and crawled out. Grofield passed him an M-16 and told him to follow. Fog had crept over the valley and sealed it in. At the perimeter, a guard spread the concertina and handed over a commo wire and said, "Follow it." It was impossible to see more than ten feet away. Running the wire through his palm, Stonehands silently walked through the fog, Grofield a close step behind. Two hundred meters beyond the fire base they reached a foxhole big enough to accommodate one man.

Smith challenged them. Grofield said, "Slick silver." Smitty told them to advance and said he was glad to leave—the fog and all. "Times I felt I wasn't alone," he said. "Like Charley was breathin' on my neck. Creepy like."

Stonehands laid the M-16 on a sandbag. He listened till their footsteps died, then sank down into the damp hole and called in a brief commo check.

The first hour he thought about anything he could but the boy. He recalled the soldier he'd boxed at Benning, a white youngster with a boy's face and a man's body, the one he was afraid to hit because where he came from blacks didn't hit whites. He'd knocked him to his knees, then held him from going down until the referee urged him to a neutral corner so the count could begin. Later the soldier had congratulated him, had shaken his hand and smiled affably as if they were now friends.

Stonehands thought he heard footsteps nearby somewhere in the damp night. He concentrated, trying to locate the sound, but heard nothing. The fog-heavy air quelled sound. In this soup Charley could walk up on him before he'd hear anything. He'd heard of soldiers going crazy at a listening post but figured they just didn't have strong minds or had just had enough of combat. Maybe, like his buddy Howkert, they were merely looking to escape.

He missed Howkert, Howkert the reader who would quote Camus and Sartre, the hippie who'd been drafted, who'd come to 'Nam with a what-the-hell shrug and a medic's bag and more guts than sense. "Why not?" he'd said. "I hear the dope's good." He had a way of seeing things that made the lunacy of war seem absurdly logical—like the old wood carrier they'd stumbled upon on the way to Dak Chat, an old man who stepped on a toe-popper, a mine meant to shatter the foot and ankle. Howkert had treated the wound and called for a dust off. As they waited, he'd asked the interpreter to ask if the old man was authorized to sweep minefields, if he held a union card. The interpreter said he didn't understand. "That's the trouble with this country—no unions," Howkert had said.

Howkert hadn't deserted because he was a coward. One thing Stonehands and the others were certain of was that Howkert was brave. But he'd deserted. What would he have thought of the boy who'd lost both limbs on the left side—both, so that no matter what aid he used to walk, he would always list to the right. How would Howkert have viewed it?

A noise distracted Stonehands, indistinct, but sound nonetheless. He was sure, so certain that he pressed the rifle butt into his shoulder and looked out over the barrel. Something was out there, an animal, a deer or wild pig. But the sound was gone, and eventually he lowered the m-16. This hadn't stopped being a forest just because of the war.

The fog was hypnotic. His eyelids drooped from staring into the dark. To keep alert, he tried to recall every movie he'd ever seen. That proved tiring. In the distance five-hundred-pounders fell to the west somewhere over Laos—Operation Arc Light. He counted explosions, seven in all, dropped from b-52s so high up their engines were silent.

"Think strong," Stonehands muttered as he cranked the field phone to make a commo check. The voice on the other end seemed uninterested. Anything out there? No, nothing, except fog and . . . noise. "Nothin'," Stonehands reported. That was the last human sound for another hour.

He remembered on the march to Hai Drong—the arvn soldiers taking over the prisoner, slapping him and shouting. The vc, helpless to protect himself, had balled up on the road. His enemies had merely seen that as an excuse to use their feet. They kicked the side of his head as if practicing soccer, straight on or sideways with an instep or backward with a heel. His squad mates, ashamed that they'd handed over the prisoner, talked about shooting the arvn soldiers and turning the prisoner loose, but that was crazy talk. Still, they were ashamed and angry. You could see it in their eyes. Perhaps that's why they'd taken to the boy so quickly—to make up for their shame.

But the boy had only brought them more shame.

Stonehands turned his attention to what he thought was movement in the fog, a swirling current. A wind. A sound. No, just imagination. Think strong. Stay awake. As a boy he'd memorized facts about presidents. His mother had bragged on him to her friends, called him into the kitchen to show the skeptics, especially Naomi Slaughter, the county Mrs. Know-Everybody's-Business. Learning facts was a trick, but they'd stayed with him. Now he drew them up—Andrew Jackson, birth date March 15, wife's name, wife's name?—Martha, no, Mary. Rachel—yes. He wasn't sure. Jackson followed by Van Buren. No one knows about him. Next was Polk. No, Tyler.

Again he heard something moving out there and had a passing desire to call out. He choked the rifle stock and listened but heard only his breathing and an annoying sound in his ears. At first he couldn't figure out where the sound came from, then realized it was in his head. It was an alarm.

As the animal circled, Stonehands, keeping his M-16 ready, wheeled in time with it. They moved cautiously like strangers testing a dance step. It coughed, not a cough exactly, but something low and guttural that seemed to vibrate out of its belly. Each of its circles became more attenuated. Though it was mostly shadow, Stonehands could identify its shoulders and head with small half-moon ears.

He checked the safety, squeezed the rifle, thinking to use it— just shoot—but that presented a different set of problems. The enemy was somewhere, a regiment perhaps, hiding in shadows, or maybe they were ghosts. Maybe all of this is shadows or, as Howkert had said, shadows without essence. If so, what is the tiger? Doesn't matter. He'd see if a ghost bleeds.

Stonehands listened to its breathing, fast and heavy, double his, perhaps. He appealed to God that it didn't make sense, his dying this way, that he'd come to fight Charley, and if he was to die, Charley should do it. Strong mind, he thought, and over and over repeated in his mind the names—Tyler, Polk, Taylor; Tyler, Polk, Taylor—like a novena.

On tottering knees, he stood up to look around. He considered calling the command bunker. And say what? There's a tiger here. What could anyone do? They'd just think he was scared. Hell, he was.

It seemed gone—a hallucination, perhaps, as the boy might have been, and the prisoner and Howkert. What did Smitty say? Felt he wasn't alone. Alone gets to you. Causes delusions. A man could imagine anything, seeing what he'd seen in 'Nam. That boy might show up in the Smokies looking for a home, another shadow looking for its essence.

The animal materialized again, a vague shadow. Some initial fear gone, Stonehands waited, rifle at the ready. Twice it stepped from and retreated back into the fog. The third time it appeared, Stonehands felt an odd sensation, a knowing of sorts. He knew for certain it was a she as she circled.

He recalled an encounter on a trail near his home when a similar sensation had guided him to a deer trapped between a tree and a boulder. He'd talked to the deer gently to slow its struggle until he'd freed it. It'd stood, dazed, its bulblike eyes staring at Stonehands until he flapped his arms and sent it scurrying into the brush. But this was no whitetail deer, or even an ordinary tiger.

The beast stopped. Stonehands tried to swallow, but his mouth and throat had gone dry on him. She inched so close that the feel of her was on his flesh. His skin prickled as if she'd brushed him. Be quick, be strong. Taylor, Fillmore . . . Pierce. Her flicking tail grazed his cheek. It was like the touch of an icicle. In the next instant, before he could recover, she retreated into the fog.

He took a deep breath and blinked. He recalled the tale of the princess, the restless spirit of the tiger that must leave one behind to assure a way into heaven. No legend. Just an animal, a big one. He wondered why he hadn't shot her and if she would return. He didn't have to speculate on that question long. All he had to do was look over his shoulder.

She faced him, opened her broad mouth and bared her teeth without uttering a sound. How she'd gotten behind him he had no idea, but she was there, and he could taste the animal smell, see the vapor of her breath swirl in the fog. He pointed the M-16 at the triangle-shaped nose, which was so close now he could see it move as she breathed. What amazed him most was her enormous head, like a moon with tufted ears. Time orbited around such a creature.

Neither he nor the animal moved. A thought occurred to him, something said about Armstrong and the moon, how a man could effortlessly break any earthly jumping record, but the results of a leap were unpredictable because he couldn't control his own body away from Earth's gravity. That was how Stonehands felt. He couldn't miss, but he couldn't pull the trigger either.

Then, as if unburdening herself of a great heaviness, she dropped to the ground no more than a foot from the foxhole, yawned once, and stared away from him into the fog. Her breathing was slower now, and from inside her rose a deep rumbling purr that prickled the hair on his arms.

He forgot everything but her. There was no sense of the world, no sense of the past or the future. Just his breathing and her rumbling. Occasionally she'd flick her tail. She was so near he could reach out and stroke her. How would she react?

She lay calmly beside him. Relaxed now, he recited presidents' names all the way up to Grant and explained how Mark Twain had found Grant living in poverty. He described the boy with no left arm and half a leg, the vc they'd captured, and explained how Howkert had gone over the wall to be with a boom-boom girl in Quang Ngai, a girl he'd planned on running away with — though there was no place to run when you were a six-foot-two-inch American, a deserter.

Sometime later she rose into a crouch, her powerful legs locked, ready. He held the rifle but had no intention of shooting. Her body twitched. She flicked her tail once again and an instant later bolted into the fog.

What would he tell his squad? Who would believe it?

A roar broke the stillness. Then a man dashed by, chattering like a lunatic in Vietnamese, followed quickly by another. A third North Vietnamese tripped on the parapet and toppled into the foxhole, his AK-47 striking the side of Stonehands's helmet. Stonehands gripped the soldier by his neck, said he was sorry, then with a powerful twist of the hands, snapped the cervical cord. He heard more soldiers emerge from the fog and laid the dead soldier aside to ring up base camp.

He whispered into the mouthpiece, "Jus' put ever'thing right on top'a me."

He cloaked his shoulders with the dead man and sank down into the pit. He heard the distinct pop, a mortar round leaving the tube. A moment later the ground became a flash pot; the sound traveled through his bones; he felt a stabbing pain in his right eardrum. He clasped the dead man, closed his eyes, and prayed.

It was still dark, but not pitch-black as before. The air smelled of nitrate. The ground remained immersed in fog, and smoke hung just above the fog, trapped by the dense net of limbs and leaves. He'd lost sense of time and fact. The barrage could have been ten minutes or two hours. He couldn't say. He listened for evidence that the enemy was gone or still there—something, a sound, but there was nothing.

He slowly rose up. The dead man on his shoulders was a painful weight, but one he was grateful for. As he readied to toss the body off his back, he felt it lift away. He hoped for a bullet to the head, a quick death, but when he opened his eyes and peered out, he caught a fleeting glimpse of the tigress dragging the dead man into the fogbank.

The phone line was severed, so he waited until dawn to crawl out of the foxhole. When at last sunlight infiltrated the forest, he saw through the fog men lying in grotesque poses. Thin vapors of smoke curled out of the ground like spun silk. Flies appeared to do their mischief. At the edge of the trees the tigress sat staring at him, her expression bland. She lay down, rolled onto her side, and began licking her paws. He thought of the legends mentioned in the tent and grasped at last what Howkert knew the night he'd gone over the wire, what it was like to be summoned.

Stonehands walked, paying no mind to the bodies he side-stepped or the ground rent by craters or the blood that trickled from his ear. These obstacles, inconsequential parts of an aberrant world, matters of limited possibility, were measurements of a past he saw evaporating with the fog. At the perimeter, he shouted the password several times, gave his name, said he was coming in and told them not to shoot. The platoon swarmed about him, patted his back, and asked what had happened. Drammel told him his ear was bleeding, said it without stammering.

The lieutenant pushed his way to the front. "How many?" he asked.

"Sir?" Stonehands looked uncomprehendingly at him, shook his head and grabbed Donatello by the arm.

"Easy, pal," Donatello said. "We thought you'd bought it—*chet roi.*"

"Where's the cub?" Stonehands asked.

"Hey, Bro . . ."

He lifted Donatello off his feet and stared into his eyes. Donatello pointed to a nearby bunker.

Stonehands swooped the cub up and walked toward the woods, his long strides devouring earth. The lieutenant ordered him to stop, but Stonehands paid no attention, and when Halverson caught up and told him to go back, Stonehands merely shook his head. Donatello hurried behind, telling him to put the cat down, that it wasn't his. Stonehands fired a single glance that sent Donatello reeling backward. No one made any further attempt to stop him. At the wire he threw his rifle aside and a few steps farther disappeared into a fogbank at the edge of the forest.

At the inquiry Donatello claimed Stonehands had returned a week later and caught him by surprise in the latrine, just appeared out of nowhere with the cub in his arms.

"What did he want?"

"To have me tell his mother he wouldn't be coming home."

"That's all?"

"That's all, sir."

"Anything else you'd like to add, soldier?"

"No, sir." Donatello looked at his squad mates. He swallowed. "Yes, sir. His eye was on the woods. He kept watching like someone who might miss a bus, worried like. Something kept moving back and forth in the shadows. I can't be sure, but I think it was a tiger."

"But you aren't sure?"

"No, sir."

The board—a colonel, a major, and two captains—looked at one another. Saying soldiers love to make up stories, the colonel dismissed the inquiry. Officially Stonehands went mad in the A Shau Valley, was missing in action and likely dead. That's what Donatello later told Stonehands's mother.

Brief facts: In the thick forests of Southeast Asia, the black and gold striping of the Bengal tiger serves to make the great cat virtually invisible to the human eye. Occasionally a hunter stalking one ends up being the prey. Several official reports from Vietnam spoke of encounters with tigers, especially among grunts who humped the mountainous rain forests. A Marine was once dragged from his foxhole near the DMZ in 1966 but fought the animal off with a K-bar knife. In 1969 Army PFC Michael Mize was dragged away by a Bengal while standing watch at a listening post west of Pleiku. His remains—a skeleton, some shredded flesh, and his dog tags, upon which dangled a tiger's claw— were found the next day. Walter "Stonehands" Harvey is one of 1,568 missing in action still unaccounted for. A neutral investigator sent to account for MIAs heard rumors of a giant running in the forests with a tigress. Laotians had seen them playing in the streams, splashing one another like children at play. They couldn't say if the man was black or not. He was a giant. Wasn't that enough?

The Cat in the Cage

Inside the earthen walls and thatch roof the air was pleasant, if not cool. The drive up in Vietnam's tropical heat had been arduous, and Calvin Widerly was glad to be out of the sun at last. He smiled as he slowly seated himself on the woven mat. A tall, stoop-shouldered man of seventy-two, he found it uncomfortable no matter how he positioned himself. He was unused to sitting cross-legged on a floor, but he thought it best to try and minimize his size. His son, he thought, would probably have felt the same way.

He watched Mai place a ceramic teapot and cups on the table. Bowing politely, she sat opposite Calvin and poured tea in his cup, then did the same for the interpreter, Tran Van Dao, and herself. Like the others Calvin had interviewed, she seemed shy yet curious, not at all hostile or resentful. He liked her already, although other than offering an initial greeting, she'd not spoken.

The dirt floor was swept and the room was clean. The air smelled faintly of cinnamon and nectar. On the table Mai had placed flowers. Hibiscus, Calvin figured, from what little he knew. He wondered if this was out of habit or in honor of him.

He said to Dao, "Tell her that her home is very nice."

As Dao spoke, Mai listened and smiled but didn't respond.

Calvin thought she was too petite, too delicate to be the mother of three teenage boys. But she was indeed their mother. He'd met the boys before being invited into the hut, youngsters with broad smiles and inquisitive eyes who had run off to play whatever games boys played here. And she'd scolded them as mothers scold sons, as his wife had scolded their own son.

"Will she talk now, Mr. Dao?" Calvin asked.

"Oh, yes, sir. She talk now."

The interpreter motioned with his hands for her to begin. At first she spoke tentatively, but gradually more swiftly in tonal syllables. The language, utterly lost on Calvin, sounded lovely in a singsong way. As she spoke she looked at the interpreter, but Calvin, looking for signs of truth, watched only her.

She paused and looked now at Calvin as Dao told him she'd been working for three years in Ho Chi Minh City, in a factory making glass roses for export. She'd cut her fingers often. The flowers were beautiful, but glass breaks. She and her husband had returned to the village, where she now worked the rice fields and he caught rare birds in the forest.

"They are happier here," Dao said.

"Tell her I'd like to do something for her if she can help. Tell her I'm an old man and my wife has died. All I have left is my daughter and two granddaughters." He thought of his daughter's comfortable brick and stucco home in Reno, warm in winter, cool in summer. "I'd like to know if she remembers a man in a cage."

The cage he spoke of, according to a one-legged Viet Cong veteran he had talked to, had been abandoned during an air strike because it wouldn't fit into the tunnels, and there had been

no time to open the barred door and lead the prisoner underground. For twenty minutes bombs had ripped the earth, up-
rooted trees, and left craters the size of ponds. At dawn when the
VC crawled out of the tunnel, they'd found nothing but barren
hillsides and blackened earth where a lush jungle had been. Untouched in the center of the devastation were the cage and the
rangy American, who pressed his hands to his ears and shouted
like a madman.

"She know a'retty what you say. Someone talk her."

"Please, tell her anyhow, the part about my wife."

The interpreter nodded and sipped from his tea. He set the
cup down and repeated Calvin's request. Mai listened. This time
she looked at Calvin. Before Dao could finish, she spoke.

"She want come America," Dao said.

She looked at Calvin expectantly.

He thought of Ho Chi Minh City, teeming with people on
foot or bicycle, and a few lucky ones on Vespas. It was to him a
city of few official details and many official denials, and the air
smelled of decaying vegetables and urine. He pictured the country he'd flown over, stretches of mud highway still effaced by
bombs dropped thirty years earlier. Who wouldn't wish to leave?

He said, "The officials warned me not to make promises of
that kind."

Hearing this, she blinked and looked away. Though she
seemed disappointed, she told Dao she understood, that it was
a hope she had, she and her husband. Calvin was limited in
amounts he could offer and had been warned that the government sanctioned his mission so long as he obeyed the rules, and
that if someone chose not to talk, he was not to press the matter. These instructions he'd received along with smatterings of
information about a man captured whom he believed to be his
son, Robert, a man who'd been captured by the side of a trail in
the Highlands in 1968 and held captive by the Viet Cong. That
soldier, like Calvin, had been a tall man.

Four former VC who'd served with the 437th VC Battalion had

told him of an American toted about for three years in a bamboo cage over spiraling jungle paths, up and down mountains from Quang Ngai to Quang Tri to Kon Tum Province. According to the vc, who'd collectively agreed to an interview in Nha Trang, that first year the prisoner had attempted escape but had been recaptured and beaten on the soles of his feet, as "bloodied feet," one had said with a grin, "hinder the most determined of men."

One of those same vc, a sergeant, had explained to Calvin how a patrol he was leading had stumbled upon an American sergeant, a very tall man, relieving his bowels beside a trail. A second American and some Vietnamese soldiers came looking for the first American. The second one was shot twice in the chest. The Vietnamese threw down their arms and fled into the forest. The tall man was forced to dig a grave with a stick and bury his dead friend. It had taken two days.

An old man living in Quo Nho'n, a former South Vietnamese soldier who'd been on patrol with Robert Widerly and Lenny Cox, confirmed that Sergeant Cox had been killed. A vc he had interviewed later in Nha Trang, a man who'd served with the 437th and was suffering from skin lesions and palsy, said he remembered a caged prisoner. He believed the captive to have been a mystic who kept bombs from falling. Again, the American had been quite tall. And Lon Truong, now dead, a vc who'd been with the 437th, had worn Robert Widerly's dog tags as a charm. In Pleiku a cinnamon trader spoke of a tall American in a cage, last seen in a village somewhere west of Chu' Pah in Kon Tum Province in 1971.

Mai lifted her cup to her lips. She glanced at Calvin, then looked at his hands as she sipped her tea. After finishing, she spoke to the interpreter.

Tran Van Dao said, "She say her husban' like American cig'rette. You have?"

"Tell her yes. In my bags."

This seemed good news—not immigration to America, but something. She spoke again to Dao.

"She remember."

Calvin tried not to feel what he couldn't help feeling, not joy or relief, but release. Here possibly was the last human, not Viet Cong, to have seen his son. He wanted the truth, if indeed such a beast existed twenty-eight years later. He would listen and fill in what she couldn't know, somehow see the story that nothing in written word or human memory could offer up. He closed his eyes momentarily, then opened them to find her waiting.

"Please, Mai, tell me," he said, "about the man in the cage."

When Tran Van Dao finished translating Calvin's request, she bowed demurely and began.

■

It was midmorning on the plateau when the soldiers slipped out of the forest, two at first, then a dozen more. The villagers, Mai among them, watched. The leader of the detachment, a razorlike man with hurried gestures, signaled and four soldiers ran to each flank before the column advanced. Diminutive figures in dark clothing, the warriors drifted in and out of shadows along the wood line. Though hard to distinguish, the object that seemed to levitate in the midst of them, swaying rhythmically with their steps, was a cage.

As the column trudged slowly atop the berm stretching from the wood line to the village, the inhabitants of Ha Ninh waited. Adolescent boys, their curious eyes tracking the progression, stood at the edge of the village. Feigning indifference, those women in view of the paddies thatched a new roof on a hut as others on bamboo mats rolled rice balls with their hands. They worked and watched furtively, their faces stoic. Mai sat beside her grandmother, who wrapped a rice ball in a palm leaf and handed it to her.

Tidings of the soldiers and the cage they carried had reached the village an hour earlier. The arrival offered a timely excuse for the men to dispose of business that had been set aside. The elder men scuttled off for Pleiku with bundles of cinnamon bark strapped to their backs, taking short, hurried steps to keep their loads balanced as they headed downriver. The younger ones went to the forest to hunt or gather where they hoped to be safe from conscription.

As the soldiers neared, nursing women gathered up infants and held them. Others filtered in from rice fields. Still more dropped whatever task occupied them and walked to the village center. The arrival of strangers demanded heed; the arrival of soldiers more so, and these carried a cage. The isolated village was populated by some sixty people, many of whom had never ventured past the second mountain peak in any direction, and only the few who traded in Pleiku had seen an American up close.

The soldiers stopped in the village square, a spot of bare, hard clay twenty meters across. They eased out from under their burden and stepped aside. Hewn from sturdy bamboo shafts and lashed with hemp, the cage stood stolid and imposing as a shrine. A hand-fashioned rope dangled in a loop from the neck of the occupant, who squatted in a corner on his hindquarters. Hand over hand, like a sloth, he pulled himself up. The roof of the cage was too low to accommodate his height, so he stooped and stared out through the bars, sighed once, and scratched the tip of his nose.

The leader directed the soldiers to disperse into the huts to search out food. One, a corporal who identified himself as Lin Phap, remained by the cage and invited the villagers to view his ward. The first line drew close as he told how the American had come to be a prisoner. He told the tale as if it were the same story he told wherever they went. Yes, they'd captured him. A terrible battle. The American had killed many, and they were kind to spare him despite his crimes. Look, look at the meanness in his eyes. As the corporal enumerated the American's crimes, the captive picked at his beard and looked skyward.

Mai peered out from behind her grandmother in order to view the cage and the corporal. What she saw surprised her.

She'd been told the captive was an American, but how could she tell? How could she be sure? Dressed in frayed pants torn at mid-thigh, he was so dark his skin was as brown as the clay the cage sat on. He appeared old, for he was bent, and his joints swollen. She slid in front of her grandmother and looked at the captive's eyes as the corporal suggested. She found nothing but two dark eyes in two deep sockets.

A woman next to Mai, Tuyet Minh, whose son had been killed by an American bomb, slid through the row of villagers, approached the cage, and spat on the American. Lin Phap laughed, as did a few villagers, but the prisoner didn't react. Mai wondered why the American didn't respond to such an outrage. Was he a holy man? Her grandmother had spoken of holy men whose concerns transcended joy or pain, men who suffered so the world might better understand the joy of not suffering.

Another woman started to throw a stone, but Lin Phap stepped between her and the cage, raised his open palm, and said that was not allowed. Lin Phap said he must shield the prisoner from torture, although some torment, mostly words, was permitted. After a last look at the captive, the villagers returned to their daily rituals. Mai's grandmother pulled her by the arm, but Mai begged to stay a while. Though reluctant, her grandmother left her, admonishing her to behave and not go near the cage.

The captive squatted on his haunches and picked at his long beard.

Lin Phap turned his nose away and said, "You stink like dead fish, Trung Si Rober' Wit'ery."

Mai listened to the corporal address the caged man in soft, familiar tones, but he used the cruelest of phrases, calling his ward a devil, a pig. And the man seemed to listen contentedly. Mai stepped nearer but was told by the corporal not to get too close, as the American had been known to stand and urinate at people, and laugh as he did so.

"He stares at the sky," Lin Phap said to her. He explained that sometimes after a period of sky gazing, "the American jumps to his feet, rants at the sky, and shakes his fists." Whenever he did this, the soldiers struck camp, as they took this as an omen.

Lin Phap said proudly that he was the fourth keeper of the cage and the kindest. He pointed to wounds on the prisoner's thighs. The American squinted at his keeper and murmured. The first, Lin Phap explained, was a vengeful master who had crushed lit cigarettes on the American's thighs and dumped buckets of human feces and urine on him, which he may have deserved, for he was an animal. Look closely, he told her. Mai looked at the man, who seemed utterly disinterested. The man in the cage rolled his head around several times, looked up, and closed his eyes to the sun. He spoke, but to what or whom, Mai had no idea.

"Don't try to understand him," Lin Phap said, "as his mind is in the sky." Other keepers, he added, had been mean as well, but he, and he alone, fed and protected the American.

The prisoner was holding on to the top of the cage and swaying when Mai's grandmother came for her. She took Mai's hand. The man was their enemy, she claimed, then added that he didn't seem like much of one at the moment. Mai asked if he was a holy man, like the ones her grandmother had mentioned. The old woman looked toward the cage. "He may or may not be," she said. "But he certainly smells."

Later, lying in her grandmother's hut, Mai turned over and over on her sleeping mat. Nothing so exciting as the man had ever happened to her village; not even bombs landing in the forest nearby had caused such a stir. She sat up and listened to her grandmother's breathing, and when it grew heavy, Mai rolled off her mat and went to the jar where they stored rice cakes. She lifted the lid quietly, only to find the jar empty. The soldiers had left nothing, not even rice cakes. She saw the cat her grandmother had bought to kill rats, still more kitten than cat and playful and soft, very soft. It was curled in the corner, staring at her.

As was custom, the village had bedded down. While the others had found shade for a nap, Corporal Phap had erected a canopy of palm leaves to lie under beside the cage. Though the sun beat down on his cage, the captive didn't seem to notice. He stared upward, his arms folded over his chest.

Mai's cat rested limply in her arms. It purred as she stroked its head and stared at Robert. If this was an American, what was there to fear? The bombs, of course, which made the ground tremble and sent her to her grandmother's mat to seek comfort in the old woman's arms. Save for Corporal Phap snoring and the caged man uttering sounds that seemed to mimic prayer, it was still, more so than at night, which was ruled by the sounds of insects and animals.

Mai advanced so slowly it seemed she'd not moved, and when at last she reached the cage, she stood ready to run. She smelled the American's strong odor and noticed his shorts where he'd urinated on himself and his talonlike nails, some broken. His matted hair that had seemed black at a distance was actually gray. His legs bore raw sores left by leeches, and his arms, back, and chest dotted by skin eruptions from mosquito bites. Lice infested him. Her throat went dry. His depravity seemed to her remarkable, nothing if not sublime. The sight of him didn't stir in her pity or even compassion, but awe. He was a holy man.

At first the man didn't react, but as she neared the bars, he turned sideways and watched her out of the corner of his eye. Mai looked first in the direction of the palm-leaf shelter where Corporal Phap snorted and shifted sides, then she scanned the other sleeping soldiers for signs of movement. With no preconceptions of what a holy man might need, or how one might react, she extended the cat for the American to see. It was an offering.

He blinked and wiped his eyes with the flat of his hand. She released the cat. It looked about and moved cautiously toward the American until it reached his bare feet. Mai waited hopefully beside the bars. The caged man shifted as the cat rubbed its side against his leg. Its tail brushed his ankle. He looked down at the cat, which touched him tentatively with a paw, sat down for an instant, then boldly jumped into his lap. Surprised, Mai watched. The cat usually ran from people, even from Mai and her grandmother. Though she heard her grandmother calling her, Mai didn't move, just waited and waited, watching until the American gradually reached out and stroked the cat's head. Mai smiled then, and ran to her grandmother.

Mai's grandmother looked about the hut and asked where the cat was. Mai didn't want to answer for fear of angering the old woman. When she hesitated, her grandmother lifted Mai's chin and demanded the truth. Mai confessed she'd given it to the American because he had nothing. He was holy and it was an offering. Wasn't that what she'd been taught to do? Mai implored. But the cat was for killing rats, the grandmother protested, then grabbed Mai by the arm and pulled her toward the square.

After the siesta, the soldiers gathered up their weapons and their booty. Some carried a chicken or a bag of rice slung over one shoulder and a rifle over the other. They'd recruited two village boys into their ranks. One was Mai's cousin, Pham, a good wood gatherer and harvester who would be sorely missed in the paddies at the next harvest. Mai's aunt wept and protested that the boy was only twelve and he'd not volunteered and he was her only son.

The old woman said sternly, "You get the cat, Mai."

Mai was scared, and hesitated as her grandmother pushed her toward the cage. The soldiers were inserting poles through hemp loops. They were raucous and banged the cage about. Didn't they know the man was holy? Didn't they know he carried her cat for good luck? Mai saw the American, the cat on his lap. He stroked it and smiled.

Uncertain of what to say, she stood in front of the cage. As the soldiers hoisted Robert, one told her to get out of the way, that she was blocking the path. The grandmother stepped forward and demanded the cat, saying that her foolish granddaughter had somehow lost it. When the corporal asked how the American got it, he looked at Mai, who shrugged and looked toward her grandmother. The old woman said they needed the cat to kill rats. The corporal nodded, not out of understanding it seemed, but impatience. Reluctantly, he told the soldiers to lower the cage.

Clutching the cat, the prisoner withdrew to the far corner as the door opened. He appeared deaf, but even if he couldn't hear, he could feel, of this Mai was certain. And the cat was soft and warm, and it purred. He petted it gently. The corporal ordered him to let go, but he didn't. The prisoner's puzzled eyes gave evidence to his thoughts as he looked about, attempting to make sense of what was happening. But it was apparent to Mai that he could not, that he had no notion of a future or memory of a past, only the cat and the embodiment of the present moment that it represented.

As Lin Phap neared him, the man in the cage squeezed the cat until it hissed and scratched his forearm. He smiled dully as the cat dug her claws into his lean flesh and drew blood. He smiled even as Corporal Phap struck him in the head with an open palm. Then the cat was free. It hissed one last time and scampered away. The corporal closed the cage door and nodded to the bearers.

Mai remained behind and watched the soldiers' progress. Once she thought the American looked back, but she couldn't be sure. She waved just in case. When the cat touched her leg, she reached down and gently gathered it up. It immediately began to purr. The soldiers marched west atop the berm until they melted into the shade of the trees. When she looked back, they and the cage were out of sight beyond the bend.

Mai knew that soon men of the village would return from the forest with wood or cinnamon bark. By morning the hamlet would again fall into the rhythms of daily life, and it would be as if the cage and the man inside had never passed through. This dismayed Mai. An occurrence such as this should be remembered, for it meant something. She felt a sadness for both the man and the soldiers who carried him.

Already women stoked wood fires to boil water for tea and rice. Smoke, black and dense, rose above the village and drifted lazily toward the forest from which the soldiers had come and into which they'd returned. It floated over the rice paddy until dispelled in the air. Mai heard her grandmother call. She stroked the cat and turned to the sound of her grandmother's voice.

■

Calvin drew himself up to stand. It was painful, for his joints were stiff and his legs had nearly gone to sleep. He pictured his son in a bamboo cage, his son who'd probably aged like a man of seventy. Three years, he thought. Again he shook his head.

"I'm thankful, Mai, that you were kind to him."

She stared up at Calvin as Tran Van Dao spoke. She nodded, then said that she wanted the cat to bring him luck, that cats are good luck, but this one was quite skilled at catching rats as well and a grandmother must be obeyed. Calvin opened his bag and rummaged for the menthol cigarettes. They were prized in Vietnam, so he'd brought along two cartons to bribe officials and was down to four packs. These he handed to Mai. She accepted them with a modest smile and asked if he cared for more tea.

"Thank you, no. I've taken more time than I should."

Dao waited patiently by the table as Mai spoke. She finished with a nod.

"She want to know if you are sad."

Calvin pictured the tall American who spent his hours staring at the sky. "Tell her I'm old, and it's an old sadness."

They stepped outside, the three of them. At once Calvin began to sweat, and for a moment, he wished he could return to the hut. But that was impossible. Here shelter was temporary, discomfort common. He stepped toward the Jeep. Through the interpreter, Mai told him to wait and hurried inside.

The smell of burning wood lay on the air. Calvin looked toward half a dozen boys, sitting on the berm, chatting. Palms blended into the wood line where the berm led to the forest, and the forest bled into the mountains. Beyond, where the sun would set in three or four hours, the mountains had turned a dark purple. He didn't belong here, just as his son had never belonged here. Too hot, too wet, too everything, even too lovely. He hoped, as Mai had contended, that Robert had somehow become holy, that a spirit existed and that it could roam the emerald forests. Mostly he hoped his son had found peace in death.

Calvin stared and imagined that last moment—the soldiers marching, the cage oscillating. A chicken on the back of one soldier flaps its wings and struggles against the cord that restrains its legs. Holding the bars of his cage, Robert sways back and forth as if to music. The soldiers pay no mind to the lunatic they are bonded to until the war ends. He travels where they go, over hilly trails, up mountainsides, through fast river currents, under the torrid sun, in rainstorms—everywhere—not a man but a charm, a holy thing, a spirit that keeps bombs from annihilating them. The soldiers laugh, celebrating their good fortune, and none notice the smile on Robert Widerly's face.

Mai came through the doorway carrying a glass rose, which she handed to Calvin. She warned him not to cut his hands on the petals.

"Mr. Dao, tell her I'll be very careful," Calvin said.

He held the flower up as he stepped toward the Jeep. The rose was fragile, and he'd have to wrap it and pack it carefully in a box with his son's rusted dog tags. He would carry the box on the flight and through customs. He'd get the flower safely home and would find a place in his house for it, a good, safe place.

A Return

Marvin Prosette stretches his arms high overhead and yells through the door screen, "Ma!" When no answer comes, he drops his arms to his side and shakes his head. He looks toward Mount Rainier, where the glacier is ringed with clouds. Signs that autumn is arriving are everywhere. The sky is a patchwork of vagrant clouds easing their way east. The fat old squirrel that lives in the oak tree has been bustling about, gathering food. Dew covers the lawn and the garden. The signs.

This is the time of life when Marvin had planned on slowing down, time set aside to shape wood on the lathe in the basement, to make chairs and stools and tables. And he would be doing that, if Casey had lived. Marvin glances at the open grave, shuts his eyes briefly, and shakes off a thought. Things to do, he reminds himself. Pears ready for harvest and no picking crew contracted as yet. It's been hard to get one in with so few pickers working.

Again he calls out for his wife. She doesn't answer. He frowns as he walks to the edge of the orchard, where he pauses to flex his arms and stretches again. Though his back is still healthy and his hands are strong, his body has stiffened. It doesn't slow him much. He still rises with the sun and at night goes down in the basement to work with wood tools. Work consoles a man. He opens the door to his toolshed, leaving it ajar for light. He comes out with a toolbox, from which he selects a pipe wrench. He rummages about for a washer, then walks to the edge of the orchard to a spigot that he's been meaning to fix. He turns the valve stem counterclockwise. In mere seconds, he replaces the washer and tightens down the valve.

He scans the orchard, looking from tree to tree—for what, he can't be certain. Then he knows. In the center of a row of lush green is the charred skeleton of a tree hit with lightning in 1969, the year Marvin nearly lost his farm and his mind, the year he began writing letters. Though he should have done so long before, he has never had the will to cut the tree out.

He returns the toolbox, then looks beyond the shed, past the edge of the house at the rough lines and divots dug to hold footers—the grass-covered trench that outlines what remains of the plumbing to the cottage that never was. He'd wanted to clean out the area many times, but there was a conflict between his wanting to and having the will to do it. Twice he had started to but simply couldn't finish. An old floor joist, sun-bleached and gray, lies on a diagonal. Beside it is a berry bush, mostly twig, that looks more like a spool of rusted barbed wire.

It was in 1970 or '71, he recalls, that the bush picked that spot to grow. He was frantic then, writing letters, some of them angry demands, some pleas for mercy. He wrote to the North Vietnamese negotiators in Paris, to the State Department, to the president. He was called a traitor in the Seattle paper, accused of giving aid to the enemy. His name was linked with Jane Fonda's. A paper in Portland called him an activist. But he was just a father with a son who was missing in action. He wanted to know why his son was over there, wanted a straight answer to that, and he wanted to find out where his son was being held if he was a prisoner of war. He wanted America out of Vietnam because he wanted his son to come home. Yes, he'd marched. His neighbors whispered, he knew, but he lived a good distance from any of them, and they could say what they wanted. It was his boy, not theirs.

Marvin looks at the house and wonders what is taking her so long. He needs something to occupy his mind, some quick piece of work. He doesn't want to reflect, but the more he resists memories, the more they intrude. He looks at the bush. Near it, the freshly excavated grave, the most difficult hole he has ever dug, is ready to accept the remains. Remains—a cottage, a grave, a son. Though machinery and help were available to him, Marvin dug the grave by hand. He felt it must be done that way for him to preserve connections.

He remembers the spring breeze and a plumb bob weaving above a footer and Casey rolling out a carpenter's string. A screen door slams and Katherine stands over Marvin with four glasses of lemonade on a tray. Behind her, a head of soft blond hair bobs as Paula emerges seemingly from a vapor, her teeth glistening like costly china as she smiles her forever young smile. Casey sweeps her up into his arms and points with pride as they seemingly glide from room to room of the cottage that is only footers, floor joists, and their imagination.

This, too, Marvin should have dug up.

How ironic, he thinks—to dig up memories means to bring them to life again, and to bury them means . . . what? He runs his fingers through his ashen hair. Memories to be buried. No. They will be buried with him. He replaces his hat. Again Marvin is reminded that there will be no rain this morning, just as there was no rain last night, just as there'd been clouds for days, but no rain. He has a sense about such things, believes a man can understand the world if he isn't always fighting it. The world is a fact, and you cannot fight a fact. He knows this too well.

He stops under a tree full of pears. The trees and the work, grafting and cross-pollinating, nursing saplings and culling out the weak, are what he has—the trees, the fruit, the work, and Katherine. Before, when Casey was alive, the trees and fruit were connected to that other world, the potential world, that landscape of possibility that encompasses strange and wonderful miracles to come, posterity, an infant suckling a finger it mistakes for a nipple, the spit-bubbled smile that is just the expression of gas pain, a reincarnation of himself and his son.

Marvin plucks a pear, a fine specimen, and holds it in his lacquered palm. He drops it into the pocket of his overalls and tilts his hat until the brim covers the lines on his weathered face. The pear is for Casey, the son he sent off like a stranger, sent off without a hug or a kiss, sent off as a result of the boy's own poor choice. For fifteen years Casey was missing in action, and for fifteen years Marvin lived on hope and letter writing.

He remembers a storm, announced by a curtain of lightning that marched down the valley. Casey, seven at the time, sat at the window, mesmerized by the brilliant flashes. Thunderclaps shook the house. It was harvest time, and the last thing Marvin wanted to come his way was a storm. He stood helplessly beside his son and watched the cold, driving rain pelt the orchard and knock pears to the ground. Soon much of his crop floated in puddles of water. When Casey asked what made the storm, Marvin said that bad luck made this one.

With his hand touching the pocket containing the pear, he goes to the porch. A patch of brilliant sunlight engulfs the yard. He clears his throat and looks into the gray void behind the screen. "Kate! Ma, we hain't got all day!" he calls into the darkness.

The screen door squeaks open and slams. On the porch Katherine stands in a pastel green cotton dress, white gloves, and soft-pink hat. As she steps down, she seems ethereal, her face in shadow under the porch roof, her skirt iridescent in the sunlight, and the sight summons a memory of her when they were young and Casey was a toddler—how she could be mother by day and lover by night. In daylight she is Kate, wearing the pearls Marvin had given her on their tenth anniversary.

"Roddy Shay called about gettin' you a pickin' crew. That's what took me so long. Marvin, you could've worn something . . . well, nicer."

He looks at his overalls. "Didn't we agree?"

"Agreed we wouldn't make it mean something to others. That's what we agreed on, Marvin. That's what we said."

"I'll have work to do when we get back. I hain't diggin' about in a suit."

She steps down. As he takes her thin arm in his, Marvin looks at it, her skin porcelain white, dappled with age. They pass by the new Buick and walk to the pickup, a '53 Studebaker, kept together by screwdriver, wrench, and Marvin's uncanny sense for things mechanical. The same truck was the chariot young Casey used on his first date and the same vehicle that carried Marvin and him in silence to a train station in 1968, more than fifteen years ago.

Marvin opens the door for Katherine. "Won't be long now, Kate," he says.

They drive in silence, a wispy trail of dust stalking the pickup as it bounces over the rutted surface of the narrow road. The last of the clouds has vanished. Sunlight spraying through the boughs of the elms on the roadside casts bangles on the roadway.

Katherine, fanning herself with a magazine, says, "I'm not angry with her anymore. Not since the letter. Funny how when I think of Casey . . ." She pauses and looks out. ". . . I think of her. Do you?"

He looks past the windshield. Not angry, he thinks? What she means to say is don't blame, too late for blame now. He's reminded of his own passion. He pictures Paula, hands moving like small birds as she talks, expressive, vital, but delicate—blond with hazel eyes and translucent skin, mouth always opened in a smile. She looked frail and harmless standing next to Casey. They'd met in the bleachers of a WSU football game. Casey had broken an ankle and was in a cast. He had brought her home one weekend that winter, then for spring break.

"No. No point." He looks at Katherine, her head jerking as the pickup lunges over the back road.

"Slow down, Marvin."

He eases his foot off the accelerator. "Did you write her about Casey like you said?" he asks.

Katherine looks down and whispers her answer. "Didn't see much purpose in it. We hardly knew her."

"No. We didn't much know her."

Marvin recalls the summer Paula stayed for three weeks. Casey gave up his room and slept on the couch. The second night Marvin heard the creaking and knew. He could hear Katherine breathing. She, too, had been awakened. He started for the room, but Katherine pulled him back by the shoulder and placed her hand over his mouth and whispered no. They lay each night for three weeks and listened until they heard the sound of Casey's footsteps returning to the couch. Then they slept.

Katherine takes off her gloves. "If her parents hadn't sent her away."

"Kate, it's done and over."

Katherine nods and fans herself with the magazine.

The truck's engine coughs. "I better get on the carburetor. Maybe we should get a new truck. I've been thinkin' about one."

Katherine folds the magazine on her lap. "It's a fine truck. You may not understand one of those new ones."

"I think I could figure one out okay."

"You haven't figured out the Buick. Marvin?"

"Buick's different; it's a car." He looks at the expression on her face and turns cold. "What?"

She bows her head. "You feeling anything?"

"It's a long time," he says and glances at Mount Rainier. What was left to feel? He'd let his feelings go with only a cold handshake. That was yesterday a long time ago, wasn't it? Vietnam fell in '75, and Mount Saint Helens erupted in '80. He vaguely remembers ash blanketing the ground and car hoods, but he clearly remembers the scene at the American embassy as Saigon fell. That he remembers vividly, and the bitter handshake he'd given his son.

Even now Marvin can't understand the bitterness he'd held in his heart over his son's rash decision. Casey returned to wsu that fall, but Paula didn't. Letters were exchanged—pregnancy, miscarriage—irreconcilable, her parents had said. A big definite word, bitter and accusing. They kept her from school and from Casey, who dropped his courses. He was flunking, offered no excuses, just said he was sorry. A shower came that night, and Casey went out in the rain-chilled air to dig up the footers. Marvin went out to stop him. They exchanged heated words.

"We're almost there, Pa."

Marvin can't bring himself to look at her.

The train station comes into sight, not a station but a dock, a covered platform with two benches and a ramp where farmers receive freight and ship their goods to market. Buster Carter and his two boys are waiting on the dock, their pickup backed up for loading. Marvin backs the truck in place next to the Carter pickup.

Marvin checks his watch. They are early. He turns to face Katherine. She touches her lips with lipstick, and blinking, touches up her eyelashes with the back of her index finger, trying to rid the trace of a tear. Marvin places his rough palm over the back of her hand.

"We'll be home soon enough," he says, rubbing the sleeve of her dress. "You'll feel better then."

"Aren't you feeling it?"

"You do the feeling." He had no room for feeling, not for years, not even when the notification arrived that Casey's remains had been identified. This was followed by telegrams and phone messages urging Katherine and him to meet the airplane. Flags and brass and drums — ceremony. He'd seen just such a ceremony on television. Eight airmen carried an aluminum casket down the ramp of a C-130. A band played a fugue. A senator, an elected official who never knew the soldier in the casket, spoke words molded on the same rhetorical models that such men used to send boys to their deaths. All the while the senator spoke, the father of the soldier in the coffin stared unblinkingly at the casket. The look in his eyes is what Marvin most remembers, that and the twenty-one-gun salute. How many letters had that father written? And what had he gotten in return, but a ceremony and remains?

"Corrine says what we decided is barbaric."

"Your sister is his aunt. You and I are his parents. We've been over it."

She looks away from him and falls silent, as she usually does when they broach the subject. What other subject has there been for fifteen years? He's thankful for the silence. He recalls how quickly the draft notice came, Casey and Arnie Chadrock receiving letters the same day. Arnie, after two years at Fort Polk passing out boots to new recruits, went to the university. A lawyer now, he's married to Chrissy Stops and practices in Yakima. Who decides such things? Who lives, who has children? Marvin asked that question in dozens of letters. How did Casey get separated from his platoon?

Before dawn, one morning shortly after Casey dropped out of college, Marvin heard a horn, and the front door open and close, then tires churned up gravel in the driveway. Casey left to be inducted, left without even saying he'd joined, until after the fact, one phone call to tell them where he was. In uniform, sixteen weeks later, he returned for a five-day leave. He'd changed, not in appearance, but in the way he measured objects with his eyes and the way he measured words, his own and others'. He was sad but seemed resigned to the fact that Paula was out of his life. He wouldn't talk about it. But he did talk about the storm that had destroyed most of the pears so many years before. He told Marvin he'd thought it was the end of the world, that it was how he imagined the world ending. But the world ends one life at a time. Who decides when a boy's world ends?

Katherine has been talking, but Marvin, deep in thought, hasn't heard her. She's looking at him. He doesn't look back.

She says, "The speeches . . . I don't want all of that. I told Corrine. But I've been thinking, and she's right. We should have something, the minister reading over him."

"I think it'll rain tonight," he says.

"You're a stubborn man, Marvin." Katherine puts her lipstick away and wipes at a tear. "Yes, probably rain."

In the distance the coming train rumbles. A groundswell of vibration builds on the tracks. Marvin steps out of the cab, walks around, opens Katherine's door. She pauses long enough to wipe her cheek dry, then takes his arm, and they walk to the bench, Marvin thinking words: "identified," "regret," "entitlement," "formal and proper," but the word that cuts into him is *remains*.

The sound of a train, by itself, stirs nostalgia, but this one more so. He'd sat on this very bench with Casey, wanting to speak of something close to the heart, but in the end they talked about pears and Rainier and how Casey would miss the seasons. Marvin shook his boy's hand and wished him luck, then walked him to the train. That moment was the future and the past and the present, and everything that would follow was already set in motion by what had been. He told his son to come back. Letters came instead, followed by more letters and anger and frustration and the year of protesting and people saying he'd gone crazy and some saying he was unpatriotic, years of waiting, corresponding with anyone who might offer hope.

Buster Carter waves. "Ya pickin' up, Marv?"

Marvin lifts his hand in a half-wave, two fingers protruding, and nods. He can't elaborate. Buster's boys, all but one, were too young for the draft, and Ned, the eldest, went to college and took four years of deferment.

"Me too," Buster says. "Me an' the boys. New generator. You?"

Marvin feels something rush to his throat to clog the words. He gulps. "No generator, Buster."

"If ya need help, me an' the boys'll be . . ."

Marvin feels Kathcrine's hand on his forearm, her fingers kneading the sinew.

Wheel grinding against rail, the train hisses to a stop, the air still and heavy with the smell of diesel oil, solvents, and livestock. A mockingbird screeches overhead. Two men, a bowlegged conductor and an officer in uniform, step down from one of the cars.

"Mr. and Mrs. Prosette?" the conductor asks.

Marvin stands to his full height. "Yes."

The conductor wrestles with a lever on the car facing the platform. The door slides open. Marvin holds Katherine's hand as she clutches her throat with her other hand. She leans her weight against him. He slips an arm over her shoulder.

The captain steps inside the boxcar and seconds later is back in front of Katherine, in his hands a flag. Marvin stares at the silver bars, a ball of melted wax hardening in his throat. Fifteen years earlier, when it happened daily, when it was a war, a sergeant might have been assigned to such duty. Marvin knows this—other boys came home that way.

The officer says, "Mr. and Mrs. Prosette, on behalf of the President of the United States of America and the Department of the Army, you have our deepest sympathies."

His brass catches a ray of sunlight, and the glare renders his face a shadow. Marvin does not hear the words; his attention is on the aluminum casket resting on a gurney. The captain finishes his speech and asks if he can offer something more in the way of help. Marvin clears his throat and looks at the officer. From the corner of his eye he sees Buster Carter and his sons. He reaches in his pocket and touches his fingers to the pear. He pulls it out. "Here," he says. "It's for you."

The officer takes the pear and examines it. "Thank you, sir. Is there something more I can do?"

Marvin realizes Buster and his sons, grown men now, are approaching. He looks at Katherine, who holds the flag to her breast. Marvin wants to hear words about his son, nothing abstract. He wants to know how his boy spent his last days, if he felt terror or thought of home at that last moment. But the captain can't provide them. Who can? He'll bury bones, but no hole is deep enough for memories.

The taste of acid is strong in his mouth. His knees are rubbery. He can't move. There is much to do. The footers for the cottage and the berry bush must come out, a sapling must be planted to replace the one struck by lightning, the boy must be buried and grass planted over the grave, and Marvin must call the minister to say some words to sanctify the moment. But how can he when he can barely move his tongue?

"No," he answers. It is a rigid no, spoken without malice.

Plateau Lands

Glenn sits up on the edge of the chaise, closes his book and rubs his eyes. He's not sure what awakened him. Perhaps the sudden drop in temperature; perhaps the thunder, or an elusive dream. He watches lightning march in columns from the west and breathes in the air, pungent but fresh. The hot August air in the Phoenix basin invites such storms, powerful, thundering storms and warm winds, then icy rain.

An insistent *ring, ring* filters through. He hurries inside to grab the receiver and shouts, "Hello." He's about to cradle it when a voice says, "Kaiser Roll?"

Glenn's throat goes dry. It's Mel. He sees him as he last saw him, the prosthesis leaning against a chair, Mel rolling a sock off to rub his stub, pink and violet and granulated. Glenn remembers the recent news brief, Mel on the small screen limping to a podium, ready to deliver a speech.

"We've got to talk. You, me, Dodrey, Mullen. Went through some heavy things, didn't we?" Mel says.

"Talk?"

"Remember Dickerson?"

Glenn pictures Dickerson seated on a boulder, arms folded over his chest, his face fearful but determined in its defiance. What, he wonders, would have happened had Dickerson taken the point with no argument when Steinbrenner told him to.

"Guess he never got it together when he came back. A street person in New Orleans—imagine," Mel adds. "Got cancer. He's dying. Made wild statements about 'Nam. Delusions of a homeless black man gone sanctimonious. Know what I mean, ol' buddy?"

"Statements?"

Glenn imagines what Dickerson is avowing. And the others? If tracked down, what might they say? He feels like a high-wire artist watching the dismantling of his safety net several stories below.

Mel says, "I'm flying in to see you, into Sky Harbor."

"What for?"

"I'm running for office. I've got a lot invested here, and I'm in a position to help guys like us."

Glenn wonders why so much ambition in one family?

"Mel," he says, "I'm a family man."

"We're all family men. I need your help."

Glenn hesitates. He wishes he could hang up, wishes he'd not picked up the phone. "Mel, it was a long time ago."

"Are you hearing me, Glenn? I'm the one who lost a leg. You came home without a scratch."

Before Glenn can speak he hears Mel lay down the receiver and tell one of his campaigners to handle the details. A woman's cigarette-deepened voice comes on the line and tells Glenn what flight he is to meet. "Mel's eager to see you. He's not too busy for an old friend. Were you there when he won the Silver Star?"

"I was."

She offers a pleasant good-bye and hangs up.

Outside, the threadlike paloverde leaves whip fiercely against the block fence. A breeze ruffles the curtains. He wishes the storm away. It reminds him of the closetlike rain forests. Rain splatters forcefully off the tiled roof as it had in Quang Ngai Province, where the sky smothered the ground — no lightning, no thunder, just rain — plateau lands smelling of decay, infernal heel-sucking mud, the tedious *thip, thip* of rain on a poncho hood. The land had seemed in a state of continual oxidation and the clay beneath his feet like rust.

Glenn doesn't bother with a light, just lowers the receiver, sinks into the recliner, and stares at the phone as if at a box of serpents. After so many years ghosts come out. The walls take on a flat, doughy hue as the room darkens.

■

From the first, Mel's life was some sort of mission. Glenn met him during ROTC class at Stephen F. Austin High in El Paso. Mel was the only freshman to earn stripes. The boys crammed into a basement room to watch films of World War II and Korea. Peabody, the sergeant in charge, would light up a cigarette and tell the boys to smoke if they had them, but to keep their yaps shut about it.

With blue smoke floating through the projector light, they watched grainy films of a series called *The Big Picture*. Often as not, the projector or the film would break and they'd have a bull session, Peabody's favorite subjects being the torturing of prisoners of war and gonorrhea. He'd tell grisly stories about how even the bravest and toughest gave in to their captors in Korea. "How'd you like to have some Commie shove a glass tube up your dick and then break it?" None of the boys liked the idea. It scared the bejesus out of Glenn.

At other times they'd clean M-1 Garands while sitting on

bleachers as the school band rehearsed in the stadium, or they'd march about practicing left diagonal turns or right flank turns and some fancy twirling of their rifles.

Mel was gaining a résumé. His junior year saw him elected FHA sweetheart and most popular boy. Though a fair shortstop, he put baseball aside his senior year to become commander of the corps of cadets at Austin High. Glenn found the corps too rah-rah and quit after one semester.

Following graduation, Glenn had an argument with his father. Determined to make it on his own, he washed dishes at Luby's Cafeteria and survived on tamales, tortillas, and Coke, and the half-price meal he ate at Luby's five days a week. He rented a room in a ramshackle house in Sunset Heights and enrolled at UTEP as a part-time student. It was a glum existence with no light on the horizon.

Two weeks after his nineteenth birthday Glenn received his draft summons. He wasn't surprised. That was the way things were going. He went with a few friends to a bar in Juárez. Mr. Haughman, his high school history teacher, showed up at El Submarino and bought the first round.

Mel happened to be there with two frat brothers from the university in Austin. Mr. Haughman mentioned a rumor about Mel's father being involved in a scandal, bad business from top to bottom, connected somehow to rezoning and illegal land purchases.

During the evening Mel swung onto the seat next to Glenn and set a fresh Carta Blanca in front of him. "Hear you're goin' to 'Nam," he said.

"Not if I flunk the physical," Glenn answered, though it was unlikely he wouldn't pass.

Mel shook Glenn's hand. "Good luck, Kaiser Roll." He used the nickname Glenn had picked up his freshman year at Austin High because his mom insisted on making sandwiches with Kaiser rolls instead of sliced bread. As Mel and his frat brothers passed by, Mel didn't acknowledge Glenn.

The morning he took his physical Glenn picked up the *Sun* off the front steps. Under the front-page headline was a photo of Dr. John Patrick McPherson and two columns of copy detailing his admitted crimes. Asserting that his conscience wouldn't allow him to take any other course of action, the dentist had turned on his affiliates and become a federal witness. Glenn noticed that his own dad had taken the picture.

A second photo of Dr. McPherson and his former associates coming out of the El Paso Federal Courthouse, their faces hidden behind copies of the indictments, was circulated in newspapers nationwide. Glenn called home to say he knew Dr. McPherson's son. Glenn's dad asked if the two of them were friends. "No," Glenn said, "he's popular." Glenn wasn't jealous; it was just a fact.

Mel called unexpectedly that evening to ask if Glenn wanted to join the Army on the buddy plan. Though they'd never been friendly, Mel acted as if they had been. He talked for some time and seemed to have a command of the history of Indochina. He also had a knack of inspiring belief in America's position. Hadn't Kennedy seen the need to preserve democracy there? It was the only war they had and would define their generation. What Mel described was all obscure to Glenn, but by the hour's end he was agreeing with most everything Mel contended and said that since he had to go anyhow, serving with a friend sounded like a good idea. Half convinced that they'd been buddies all along, Glenn hung up. Mel never once mentioned his father. At the time Glenn saw no irony in this, but later he would.

■

Glenn doesn't hear Angeline call out, is unaware she's home until she steps into the family room on her way to get a mop to sponge up the rain that dripped from her coat and umbrella. She shuts the sliding door and closes the drapes.

"Why're you sitting in the dark?"

He squints into the light. "Daydreaming."

She flips on the lamp and sits on the ottoman by his feet, looks at him for a moment before bending forward to kiss him. Her arms rest around his neck as she lays her cheek against his throat. She runs her finger around his ear. "You need to trim the hairs," she says. "Beautiful storm." She pulls away to look at him. "Are you okay?"

"I'm fine."

"You don't look so fine. There's nothing like a storm in the desert. It's magical."

"McPherson's coming in."

"The McPherson?"

"Mel McPherson."

"He didn't come to our wedding. I wondered why. At the class reunion he said you'd joined the Army together."

Glenn shakes his head. "I never mailed his invitation."

"Oh."

He wishes the conversation would return to small talk, more about desert storms, but it doesn't. She asks about Mel's limp, a subject Glenn doesn't care to think about, though he thinks about it daily and has for almost thirty years. He sees Mel fall to the ground, gripping his leg, blood spurting from the wound. The others of the platoon, who are firing, stop. Everything stops. That is what Glenn remembers — the moment of silence that preceded Mel's scream.

"He lost his leg from the knee down."

"Was he a hero?"

Glenn feels a pinch in the back of his neck. "Depends on who tells it, I guess." He wishes there was a concrete answer, some absolute account he could give her. "He was awarded a Silver Star."

She remains silent, studying him. They know each other too well for this. He can't look her in the eye for fear she may see into him. And what would she see first? A half-truth? Fear? To escape her gaze he walks to the door and spreads the drapes with his fingers.

"Where's Cory?" he asks. Cory, all boy, rough and loud, Cory who just this year came to regard him as the best stepfather he could have hoped for.

"Rollerblading. What does McPherson want?"

"In this rain?" Glenn feels her blue-eyed gaze as he watches water drip from the eaves.

"Not now. He was. Why are you changing the subject?" she asks. "What did he want?"

He extracts his fingers from the drapes. "A guy we served with is dying of cancer."

"I'm sorry. What's his name?"

"It doesn't matter."

"Names matter," she says.

He knows she's waiting for him to say something else, but he doesn't. In time, she sighs and goes to the wet bar, where she pours two jiggers of schnapps into two glasses and squirts lime into each—a drink she calls a Schlime. She motions Glenn over.

"Sometimes a guy'll talk to a bartender."

He'd used this line the night he proposed, told her to fix them drinks—which she did—and then he explained that a friend of his was in love with a woman with a nine-year-old boy who hated him, but the friend wanted to marry her, which might make the boy miserable and probably himself as well. After weighing this, she'd told him to tell the boy man to man what was on his mind.

"Nothing to tell a bartender," he says.

Her eyes settle on his collar. With a flick of her fingers she brushes away a piece of lint. "I see," she says and sips her drink. "Cory wants to go to the arcade later."

"Okay."

He looks out at the storm. She waits patiently as he stares out. Finally, she swallows her drink, says they need some lights on, and heads to the broom closet. When she returns, Glenn's standing in the same spot.

"His name's Dickerson," he says. "In a sense, Mel saved his life." He offers a trace of a smile, which she ignores.

After she leaves, he flips on a second lamp and picks up the book with every intention of reading, reading if for no other reason than to forget. But he can't concentrate. He keeps seeing Mel kneading that grotesque stub. Glenn feels his fingers twitch. He remembers Professor Cloverdale saying there was no relative truth regarding a fact, and nothing was at stake but the truth when the truth needed to be told. But no philosophy professors took their ethics classes in Vietnam, where the polar facts were firepower and body bags. Everything in between was as relative as the next breath or the next heartbeat.

■

For five soft days they'd bivouacked in Quang Ngai City, swum in the South China Sea, smoked dope, romped in the whorehouses, and bellyached about losing Povel, who'd matriculated. Gone. Pov, who'd looked the other way when they smoked dope or got drunk, who'd held the hands of their wounded, who'd played to their strengths. He'd done a year, made it — both legs, both arms. That was two weeks earlier.

The new platoon leader tramped into camp, gear slung over his shoulder, and caught them standing around shirtless and unshaven. He called a platoon meeting. Before he'd unloaded his gear or loaded his M-16, he told them they'd have to square away or face Article Fifteens. The Army had rules. He intended to follow them. Things would change.

After that, rumors flourished. They were operating the plateau lands of Quang Ngai Province east of Ha Tanh, a twenty-klick belt of rice paddies and hamlets, which they called villes, a lot of Local Force Charleys, snipers, and dirty. Timmons in the first squad insisted Steinbrenner had volunteered them to recon the foothills, said he'd overheard the radio message. Arbors, a spec four from another squad, said they were tethered goats, bait to draw out a division of NVA that was supposed to be in the area. Though Mel urged the squad to give Steinbrenner a chance, the men didn't trust him.

The rain started—four days, no sky. Then Dodrey, whom the lieutenant had used at point the day before and two days before that, was sent out a third day. It was someone else's turn, but Steinbrenner insisted Dodrey go up there, almost as if he wanted him to die.

To the man, the platoon liked Dodrey. The day he arrived, he'd tossed his gear outside Mullen's tent and had lain down, hands behind his head. Mullen, the bullish AR-man, came upon him resting beside the tent as if he owned Vietnam. Provoked by Dodrey's insolence, Mullen had lifted him to his feet. "Listen up, Powder Face. Get yore gear and yore mangy ass outta hea', 'less you want me to kick yore butt all the way up to yore neck," he said, gave him a look that, if it had been chemical, would've defoliated an acre of forest, then let go with a shove.

Dodrey had grinned as he threw his backpack over his shoulder. "I'll get back to you on that. Need some time to think about it," he said and walked away.

A smile blossomed on Mullen's face. "Get yore ass back here," he had said.

Soon they were inseparable. Mullen laughed at the mere thought of one of Dodrey's many pranks—like the time he smeared his lips and cheeks with lipstick and walked into Sergeant Gonzalvo's tent to tell him he was in love with him. Gonzalvo looked up and told Dodrey he wasn't getting a discharge no matter. Dodrey said, "In that case, will you marry me?" Mullen told the story to anyone who'd listen.

Saying he got first go at the ladies, Dodrey took point. He was on a berm when a Bouncing Betty shot up and landed benignly on the ground as if a dud. He looked back and winked at the miracle. But the miracle was merely a delayed fuse. The explosion tossed him into knee-high water in the rice paddy, where he floated belly-up, an incredulous, almost amused, expression cemented on his face.

■

Angeline eats quietly while Cory, excited over having found a new friend, a boy name Oliver who can rollerblade as fast going backward as forward, talks at a demon's pace. Glenn, glad for Cory's chatter, encourages him to describe the various tricks Oliver performed. "Jumped over a banister and cleared six stairs," Cory says.

"Six steps," Angeline corrects. "And I don't want you jumping obstacles. We had an agreement when I bought those. I won't have it."

Cory says he didn't jump anything. Silence falls over the table until she drops her napkin and leaves.

"What'd I do?" Cory asks.

"Nothing."

After dinner he drives Cory to the arcade. They take the Dreamy Draw to Thirty-second Street. The cliffs are wet and shiny. They roll down their windows and let the moist air cool the car. They are silent. They play a few games on a rocket simulator until Cory's friends arrive. Glenn watches. Cory's fingers are efficient and detached. As he manipulates the joystick, two friends stand with their hands on his shoulders encouraging him. Their open affection for one another amazes Glenn. When he finally loses his turn, Cory glances back and gives Glenn a look that says, This is for kids only.

Glenn absentmindedly shoots undersized basketballs at an undersized hoop. A cacophony of children's voices blends with the buzz and whine of computerized games. What, Glenn wonders, has happened to his boyhood friends? He clearly remembers those from 'Nam—McPherson and the others—but the boys he played marbles and Ping-Pong with have been wiped from his memory.

Cory picks up a basketball and swishes it through the net. Glenn asks how he did. He shrugs. Glenn suggests a double-decker cone. Cory is licking the side of his cone when he looks up at the ceiling. Glenn's eyes naturally follow. "Gotcha," Cory says and they laugh. For the moment the laughter melts away Glenn's misgivings. He says not to mention the ice cream to Angeline.

"Why's Mom mad at you?"

"She's not."

"Then why're you mad at her?"

"I'm not."

The boy rolls his eyes.

As soon as they turn in the driveway, Glenn's stomach churns. He doesn't understand himself, why he can't just prepare her for Mel. Mel, who merely wants him to help perpetuate the lie.

Angeline is in the family room watching television when Glenn opens the door. Cory rushes inside. She tells him to come give her a kiss, but he runs upstairs instead, his heavy adolescent feet thudding on every third step. Angeline hollers for him to brush his teeth.

Glenn says, "He's just at that age." He crosses the room and sits next to her. "I like my home the way it's always been," he says.

"Which means?"

He shakes his head. Early in their relationship they'd agreed it was important to talk. Silence had destroyed their previous marriages. Though he wants to talk, he's unsure what to say.

"I don't know," he says, and as soon as he does, he realizes this was the worst thing to say.

She stares back with a closed expression.

Glenn uses the banister to climb the stairs.

Cory lies on his back reading a book.

"Is it good?" Glenn asks.

Cory shakes his head slowly. "About Arthur Ashe. I only read the first page. I knew you two were fighting."

"We're not."

"You're not talking," he says. "That's fighting."

"It's relative."

"It's a fact. Didn't you tell me if something's a fact, it's true?"

"Must you remember everything I tell you?"

"Gotcha," Cory says.

"Got you," Glenn corrects.

Glenn had noticed from the first night they'd slept together that Angeline could brush her teeth longer than anyone he ever met. Tonight she stays in front of the sink for a half hour. When she comes out, he asks if she brushed away all the enamel. She crawls under the cover and lies on her side with her back to him.

"Tell me about someone from 'Nam," she says.

Keeping on safe ground, he tells her about Dodrey and the lipstick. She chuckles, flips off the light, and asks for a back rub. He kneads her back and says, "Now let's play a new game. On the count of three you roll over."

She looks over her shoulder. "Did McPherson think Dodrey was funny?"

"Mel?" Glenn feels himself shutting down again, then it occurs to him that Mel never laughed. "No."

"Tell me more," she says, "about Dodrey."

"He was irreverent. We had to burn the latrines to kill fly larvae. One day he opened a can of Vienna sausage, put one on a sharp stick, and roasted it over the flaming latrine. He had the whole squad doing it, except McPherson, who couldn't get into it."

"You ate them?" Her voice registers disgust.

"No, just tossed them down the hole. It was something crazy and American."

"You liked Dodrey?"

"Oh, yeah." Lying in bed with the person who defines love for him, Glenn can't put into words the feelings the squad members had for each other. He touches her cheek.

"Were you a good soldier?" she asks.

He considers it and realizes it's the most fitting question anyone could ask about 'Nam, one he's never been asked. "We were good."

"Even McPherson?"

"Especially Mel."

"Let's make love," she says and strokes his head where it's gone bald.

Glenn awakens driven by a dream in which his wife is walking up a winding path on the side of a hill and though he calls to her she doesn't stop. But it isn't just her, it's the hill, an incline covered with elephant grass and vine tangles where he can't follow. He sits upright and listens to her breathing. She's peacefully asleep.

He tiptoes out and goes down to the den, where he opens the curtains and sits in the recliner. The storm has receded. A few black clouds slip across the moonlit sky like stalking cats. The wet sheen covers the green branches of the paloverde. He planted that tree when he and Angeline bought the house. He wishes he could hear the desert as he heard it when he first came back, when he could pick out the chirp of a solitary cricket, when his senses were keen and the dry hot air was a calming hush. He fears something is about to sever him from his world, that tree, this house, her, Cory, the students he teaches government to.

He knows what Mel will be asking of him. Mel needs to be a hero, always needed that, but it's hard to find heroes in memories of the days that followed Dodrey's death. It's as hard to find a hero as it is to pretend there's no truth. Glenn wonders how strong the foundations are that hold his home together, how much fact his marriage can endure, how much respect Cory will have for a stepfather who has lied to cover up something terrible. His hands shake. He considers having a drink. But that won't help. Perhaps he should call Professor Cloverdale and ask him how to cast the facts in a way that won't shatter lives.

Wasn't it ethical to forgive those who went to Canada and Sweden? Weren't the same kind of young men tossed into a turmoil and asked to risk their lives and do terrible things? Can't they be forgiven their transgressions as well? How would Cloverdale, who was so quick to praise amnesty, answer that?

Glenn feels cold. He's used to the warmth of his wife's body.

Often he reaches for her in his sleep, and she nestles against him. In the morning he remembers it like a dream. He carries that dream with him throughout the day. That is fact. Glenn can prolong the lie. That is fact. Who can say how many men Mel saved? Isn't that what heroes do? What happened now seems liquid, a memory he can drown in. Can it be, like the warmth of Angeline's body, fact? Over there you wore the heat like a glove enveloping your body. It affected the mind. That is fact.

∎

The rain had lifted the night before and now it was humid and scorching. Their fatigues blackened with sweat, they humped like old men bent under the weight of their loads. There was anger in each man's step, a kind of plodding, obstinate step. After days of sloshing in monsoon rains, they despised Steinbrenner.

Their already decimated platoon took seven casualties as they moved into the foothill villages. A Cong in black pajamas popped out of a hole and fired two shots before his rifle jammed. One hit Mullen under the right jaw and exited his eye socket. The squad went full rock 'n' roll on the vc. Though he was dead from the first volley, the squad gathered around, and each man in turn shot one round into the body as the others urged him on.

Steinbrenner shoved his way into the circle and ordered them to stop, said he wouldn't tolerate barbarism. He'd heard about massacres, and nothing like that would happen in his platoon. The squad stared at the ground. Dickerson, who'd not yet shot, pointed his m-16 at the Cong's head, squeezed off a round, and said, " 'Scuse me, sir, was a ax'dent."

Steinbrenner had come to represent all that was fucked up about 'Nam. That night the platoon took a mortar barrage — four men wounded. Gonzalvo, Jones, and Smeltzer went out in body bags.

In the morning the platoon was ordered out again, and Steinbrenner gave McPherson Gonzalvo's .45 to carry and told him he was acting platoon sergeant. Glenn was promoted to leader of the Third Squad to replace Mel. Second Squad was down to four, so the lieutenant told Glenn they were part of his squad now. The unit numbered but seventeen as they climbed into the mountains southeast of Ha Tahn.

Glenn's squad took the lead and he assigned Malcomb to the point. By noon they were in vine tangles and elephant grass. Glenn asked Dickerson to take Malcomb's place. Dickerson looked down at the ground and told him no. "What?" Glenn asked. This time Dickerson looked up as he said, "No fuckin' way. You take it. Or McPherson or that fuck-up lieutenant they give us."

Glenn put out security and sent Ridgeway to get Mel. Dickerson was hardheaded, but he had never bucked Mel. Mel looked at Glenn and at Dickerson, who sat on a rock with his arms folded over his chest. Mel asked what the problem was. Glenn told him Dickerson refused to take point.

"That right?"

"'At's right, an' no cracker's gonna make me."

"Shit! They'll court-martial your ass," Mel said.

By then Steinbrenner had worked his way up the line. When the lieutenant came into sight, Malcomb said he'd stay at point himself, that it didn't matter to him.

"Don' matter nothin' to me what he do 'cause I ain't movin'," Dickerson said.

"Sergeant McPherson, is this soldier refusing an order?" Steinbrenner asked.

"Not exactly, sir."

Lieutenant Steinbrenner pointed an index finger at Dickerson, said it sounded like he was, then called Dickerson "son" and asked him to redeem himself.

Dickerson said he was no coupon to be redeemed and no son of a lieutenant either. The squad laughed.

Steinbrenner's cheeks reddened and he stepped closer. "I have the authority to shoot a man for mutiny or cowardice in the face of the enemy."

"No enemy face here 'cept yore's," Dickerson said.

"Soldier, you obey the order you were given."

The platoon knew Dickerson was no coward. When they'd been pinned down near Boun Ma Thuot, he'd saved them by carrying a belt of ammunition to Mullen despite the heavy fire.

The lieutenant looked at McPherson. "Sergeant, shoot this man."

Mel looked appealingly at Dickerson. "Look, man, I'm not going to kiss your ass. Now, quit fucking off." He held the .45 at his side and licked his lips. "Come on, Dickerson. We go back a long way. Don't do this."

" 'At's right, we go back. But he don' go back wif us. Got Dodrey kilt an' Mullen an' Gonzalvo."

Now one by one the black soldiers sat down and folded their arms over their chests. Then the white soldiers followed suit. The lieutenant looked at them. "Sergeant, I said shoot him."

" 'At's right, McPherson, shoot my black ass. Don' matter if you shoot me or some Cha'ley does. Dead's fuckin' dead, ain't it? Ask Dodrey an' Mullen."

Steinbrenner said, "Shoot. It's a direct order, Sergeant."

Hand trembling, McPherson raised the pistol level with Dickerson's head. His finger closed on the trigger. "Don't make me, Dickerson."

Dickerson lowered his gaze toward the ground and nodded in resignation. "Get it done," he said.

"It's an order, Sergeant."

Mel looked at the lieutenant out of the corner of his eye and shook his head. His arm went limp. "I can't, sir."

"You're under arrest, Sergeant," Steinbrenner said. He drew his own .45 and chambered a round.

Steinbrenner fired one round—that into the ground as he fell forward. The men gathered about and gaped at the hole in the dead officer's head. For a moment Glenn stood motionless, his pistol still aimed where the officer had been standing an instant before. His arm dropped to his side as he looked at Dickerson and said, "Go take point." Dickerson nodded and headed in that direction, but before he'd moved three steps, Mel ordered him to stop.

"They'll shoot us all," he said.

They circled about, nervous, worried. *Mutiny.* It was one thing to think of killing an officer and quite another to do it. Timmons asked what they were going to do, the question naturally directed at Mel. Turner, a sad-faced blond kid, said it was all Mel's doing.

"No," Glenn said. "We're in this together."

Mel stared down at the dead officer. When he looked up, he told them what needed to be done. When he asked if they all agreed, he looked to Glenn, who nodded. Some were at first reluctant, but gradually everyone agreed. Mel touched a finger to the lieutenant's wound, unbuttoned his shirt and crossed his heart with the blood. One at the time, each man did the same.

Mel rigged a grenade beside the lieutenant's head and hooked a wire to the pin. He took cover behind the boulder where Dickerson had made his stand. A flick of the wrist and the evidence was gone. He called battalion HQ on the PRC-10 while in the background the men fired wildly, tossed grenades, and set off Claymores.

Before he radioed for an evacuation, Mel argued that one casualty would seem suspicious. He told Glenn to shoot him in the leg. When Glenn hesitated, Mel insisted and closed his eyes. Glenn aimed for the meaty flesh of the left thigh away from an artery, but something happened, a twitch, an instant of reservation, something awful. The bullet strayed. McPherson collapsed, his knee smashed. It was left to Glenn to carry the decapitated lieutenant to the helicopter.

■

Glenn has often wondered how his aim drifted, sometimes isn't sure it was an accident at all. No matter. It was his doing, and the debt followed. That, too, is fact, or has been until now. He's not slept. He has been waiting for dawn or for a Cloverdale answer to come his way. Start by doubting everything, Cloverdale said. Glenn closes his eyes. Perhaps there's something he hasn't considered.

When he opens his eyes, he sees Angeline leaning against the doorjamb. He hadn't noticed her before and wonders how long she's been there.

"Something's invaded my home," she says.

Yes, he thinks, they are under siege, the past invading the present in the form of words from a dying man's lips. The truth impinges like an insurance agent who refuses to leave until the policy is signed. She asks if he wants company. He moves over and pats the cushion. She slides next to him, folds her arms over her breasts, and nestles her head into his shoulder. Glenn wonders what safety net is going to fall. He sees rocks below, sharp ones, that he must land on barefooted.

"Did Mel save your life or something?" Angeline asks.

"Me?"

"Is that what this is about?"

"No, Mel didn't save me. It was luck and . . ." He looks at her. There was something in between firepower and body bags, something between men who needed each other. All of them were scared, but none were really cowards. They trusted. They trusted their weapons, their skills, but mostly each other. Cloverdale would never understand trust because it's not based on doubt, yet it was clearly trust that kept them together, that perhaps kept them alive.

"Tell me," she says, bending her face closer, so near her breath stirs the hair on his neck. Her voice is not urgent.

He feels a final pang of doubt, of fear, and asks for her hand. She links her fingers with his. He looks at their coupled hands and remembers a guy in the platoon, a new guy who got wounded his third day in 'Nam. Glenn and Dodrey took turns holding the guy's hand. No name. No face. Just a guy who trusted them to get him onto a helicopter. Glenn wishes he could remember the guy's name.

They sit like that for several minutes, watching daylight filter through the curtains. Glenn sees the green branches of the palo-verde. He pictures the day he planted it, Angeline bending down as he patted the dirt around it with his hands. They made impressions of their palms side by side in the soft black soil, then stood next to each other smiling down at the mound of dirt. This, he knows, is when he must begin. He squeezes her hand gently and says, "We were nineteen . . ."

Tunnel Rat

Young people were messy then—the war, the draft, plentiful drugs. Rowe and Betty were singularly so. They'd club-hop, starting at the Pussy Cat à Go-Go, the lounge at the Flamingo, then the International, up and down the Strip, dancing, drinking, and popping uppers, then back to the Pussy Cat and him off at daylight with no sleep to work for Grady. Rowe wore a T-shirt with a Superman emblem emblazoned in red and yellow. Betty slept while he worked.

When she found out she was pregnant with his baby, she cleared her clothes out of the closet in their apartment and left behind a half-drunk bottle of tequila, a baggie of cross-tops, and a short note declaring she'd run off with Tom, a former lover. Rowe held the note, his hands ossifying as he stared at it, then his legs gave way and he collapsed into a recliner Betty's father had given him.

Rowe's mother had warned him Betty would break his heart. Now she had. Eventually he popped the note into his mouth and chewed it to a wad compact enough to swallow. He dropped three cross-tops and chased them with the tequila. He didn't bother to lock the door, just slammed it and headed into the night. One strong kick started his 650 Bonneville. He rode non-stop from Vegas to San Francisco, where he found a squalid Haight-Ashbury flat to hole up in.

Earning money under the table, he laid carpet and stayed stoned or drunk for the next two months.

Across the hall lived a self-proclaimed guru of the free love movement named Lonnie, who pushed acid and peyote. An avowed social revolutionary, on the side he interned as an entrepreneur, pimping fifteen- and sixteen-year-old runaway girls. One evening he and Rowe had a difference of opinion over a girl who said she wanted to leave if Rowe only would be so kind as to give her a ride to the bus terminal and send her back to Spokane.

Lonnie caught Sunshine in the hall with her bedroll slung over a shoulder and pulled her to a halt by her ponytail. He insisted he loved her. Rowe told him to let go. He refused, so Rowe busted Lonnie's jaw and two fingers. The girl's loyalty wasn't as unsettled as Rowe thought. She called the police. Fatigued from so much peace and love and fearing arrest, Rowe kick-started his Triumph in hopes it would hold together long enough to get him to L.A. It did.

Against the wife's objections, Rowe's Uncle Harve sheltered him in his Bellflower home. They were blood, Uncle Harve contended, no matter how Rowe smelled or how unkempt he looked or even if he was a federal fugitive, which he might be.

Rowe dialed his mother, who said his draft board had turned his name over to the FBI. He told her it was a strange world where a guy couldn't go off to mend a broken heart without becoming a criminal. She said he owed her twenty-two dollars on a phone bill she had to pay after he'd left. Rowe said he'd send the money from prison or Vietnam or Sweden. His mother said she wouldn't hold her breath.

Rowe called Grady, who informed him Betty had returned, alone, had aborted the baby, and had been dumped by Tom at the door. She was still too upset to come to the phone. Grady, who owned a construction firm, a downtown casino, and a ranch in Montana, had about half the money in the free world, but Rowe didn't hold this against him, in fact liked him though he'd made a mess of his daughter and two sons, who were a bit off-axis. On the other hand, Grady loved Rowe like a son and told him so.

"FBI's looking for me, I think," Rowe said.

"I'll hide you, put you to work and pay you under the table, double scale. I'll tell Betty you'll be comin' back. Won't bother me to see her marry you. I got a fondness for you."

"Probably won't work out," Rowe said, meaning marrying Betty. Besides he'd decided a fugitive's life wasn't for him.

"Don't worry, boy. I know people who can fix anything."

Rowe thanked Grady just the same and wished him and his daughter well. His one chance to avoid jail was to find a charitable recruiter, plead ignorance, and join up.

The recruiter looked up. "May I help you?"

"I understand you're looking for killers," Rowe said.

"Beg your pardon?"

"Killers. Men to kill Viet Cong. I want to kill some."

The recruiter smiled. "That's the best damned reason for joining this man's army I heard all week. You're a romantic, damn few of your sort left."

"Thank you."

"Ever think of the French Foreign Legion?"

"In what terms?"

The response seemed to baffle the recruiter. Rowe explained about the draft board and the FBI. The sergeant took Rowe's Social Security number and gave him a test, telling him in confidence that the score didn't matter all that much, that indeed boys who wanted to kill weren't as easy to find as one might guess. Rowe scratched down answers as the recruiter phoned the draft board in Las Vegas to tell them to call off the feds, that Rowland Thomas Hobbes was about to serve his country as a soldier in arms.

"How'd you get a moniker like that?" the sergeant asked.

"My mom did crossword puzzles instead of being a mother."

The next morning Rowe parked his oil-leaking motorcycle in his uncle's garage and thanked him for the kindness. Uncle Harve said Rowe would probably get himself killed, but maybe that was what he wanted. Rowe told him he was too young to know what he wanted, especially about something as serious as dying, but that when, at last, he found out what it was he *did* want, his uncle would be the first to hear. The recruiter picked Rowe up at 7:00 A.M.

"Well, how do you feel, Killer?" he said.

"Stupid at the moment," Rowe answered, "but I'm sure I'll feel a lot dumber later."

The sergeant seemed disappointed to find that Rowe wasn't such a romantic after all, but that revelation didn't deter him from his duty. By 3:00 P.M. Rowe was raising his right hand and mumbling words about the Constitution of the United States of America. Already he was feeling a lot dumber.

As the tailgate of the C-130 dropped, hot air funneled in and brought with it dust and a stomach-turning stench. Every face in the plane reacted. A trooper gagged. The one next to him told him to breathe through his mouth. This was Vietnam, Rowe figured, and whatever waited outside was home for however long they were here, a fact he resigned himself to.

The load master motioned for them to deplane. They hefted their gear and headed toward the rear with a sense of resolve. The big turbo props screamed as the plane readied for a quick turnaround back to Tan Son Nhut.

Rowe stared at the fallow surrounding the strip. Shielding his eyes, he gripped his duffel bag and hurried through the prop blast. The others followed. A bored-looking staff sergeant with skin like redwood bark met them at the edge of the strip and formed them into a line. A piece went off—a 155, he figured. Then the plane lunged down the runway and launched itself into the cobalt sky.

"Welcome to goddamn Cu Chi," the sergeant said. "Grab your gear and follow."

The guy beside Rowe asked where the hell they really were. Rowe shrugged. Again the artillery piece went off. They fell into step, bound for a city of tents and Quonset huts appearing much like an olive-drab ghetto constructed by a sailmaker.

"What's that smell, Sarge?" the man behind Rowe asked.

"What smell?"

"Smells like shit," the replacement said.

"You'll get used to it." As they marched, the sergeant meted out congenial in-country wisdom. The village was VC, he warned, "Men, women, boys, girls, goddamn pigs, goddamn goats, and even goddamn dogs. You can get anything there, dope, pussy, French cigarettes, a goddamn black market stereo, and things you don't want—tuberculosis, clap, and goddamn dead."

The 155 mm sent another round beyond the perimeter.

Cu Chi, the sergeant explained, had been fertilized for centuries by human shit, which accounted in part for the odor—but just in part. Headquarters sat in the middle of a lowland plain near Highway 1 atop a catacomb of tunnels dug by guerrillas. "Goddamn vulnerable to sapper attacks."

He elucidated how a new tunnel occasionally would be located and engineers would blow the opening and declare it harmless. "Once one's harmless, it's harmless no matter how many sappers crawl outta it," he said. An artillery round punctuated his every ninth or tenth sentence as if timed to emphasize his point. "If you're pullin' guard near a hole that's harmless and you see a fuckin' slope crawl out with twenty pounds'a C-4 and a goddamn detonator, it's a goddamn illusion. The whole country's a goddamn illusion. If you're bleedin' to death, it's a goddamn illusion."

The guy behind Rowe whistled under his breath. The 155 went off. The blast went through the soles of Rowe's feet.

They halted at a Quonset hut with a sign reading REPO DEPOT, and the sergeant turned them over to three spec fours, who casually thumbed through files. When Rowe's name was called, the interviewer motioned him onto a fold-out chair. The clerk's name tag read "Hoffman." An unlit cigarette dangled from his lips as he spread Rowe's file and looked at the test scores.

He studied them. "Hobbes, can you type?"

"No."

"How'd you end up in the infantry?"

"Lucky, I guess."

"You're going to find this hard to believe, Hobbes," he said, "but I'm like God, life and death right here." He held up a ball-point pen.

"I don't find anything hard to believe," Rowe said.

Hoffman lit his cigarette and exhaled. "Rifleman," he said and looked away. "Okay." He ran his finger over a list on a clipboard. "After Charm School, you'll be going to the Wolfhounds. You're lucky."

"How's that?" Rowe asked.

"You'll get to meet new people on a regular basis—*if* you live long enough." He stamped a series of forms, initialed them and closed the folder. "They've got the highest casualty rate in 'Nam."

They fed at a nearby chow tent, after which they returned to the repo depot and, with files in hand, waited for rides. A deuce and a half crunched to a halt on the dry clay, its huge tires spewing a knee-high cloud of orange dust. The driver said three mechanics belonged to "Thirty-fourth Armor." Two PFCs and a spec four tossed their gear in the truck bed. Cooks or quartermaster clerks or medics went, like the mechanics, straight to their units.

Hoffman stepped outside and lit a cigarette. "You'll remember me in a week, Hobbes," he said.

"Why's that?"

Hoffman walked away without answering. A moment later a sergeant stopped in a Jeep and got Rowe's attention. "You the one for Charm School?"

All day and all night at twenty-second intervals a 155 mm fired outgoing toward some nebulous point on the map — the Twenty-fifth's version of Western Union, thousands of dollars' worth daily. *Thaboo!* You could set your watch by the report. *Thaboo!* Sixteen paces while marching. *Thaboo!* Twenty-two normal heartbeats. *Thaboo!* Thirty-four heartbeats if exercising. A monotonous, maddening ritual, it soon became a comforting sound, a lullaby of sorts. The sound made Rowe homesick, and he thought of Betty, pictured Grady telling her she should be glad to have a boyfriend like him.

He couldn't step outside and take in fresh air. There was none, only smells he couldn't quite get used to. Each and every day somewhere someone was burning shit with gasoline. Black smoke billowed up and drifted over the compound and brought with it more stink. Rowe got somewhat acclimated to the heat and learned the different ways Charley could kill a grunt, got used to the sounds of artillery rounds and bombs and machine-gun fire at night, but he didn't adjust to the smell of urine and feces, of dust and mildew. At night he thought of Betty.

After Charm School, where he was shown a few booby traps and land mines and told the three hundred and seven painful ways to die in 'Nam, Rowe was officially ready to join his unit. He'd learned a new vocabulary — A.O., dust off, *di di mao,* boom-boom, *xin* fuckin' *loi.* Though not a bit wiser than on his first day, he was measurably more scared. And Hoffman proved right; Rowe remembered him in less than the week predicted. Hoffman was already despised, a Rear Echelon Motherfucker who swilled beer or smoked grass, watched movies, and sneaked into

the cardboard-shack village with a fistful of black-market pias-
ters to court boom-boom girls. To forget him, Rowe went to the
EM club, where he drank beer and thought of Betty.

One night Rowe met a door gunner at the club. Over his fifth
or sixth beer the gunner told a story about unloading Vietnamese
soldiers into a hot LZ near Dak To. One froze in the seat and
refused to go. The gunner claimed he shot the Vietnamese and
tossed him out when the chopper gained altitude, said it was him
or them, meaning the crew, and he didn't intend to wait until
the Vietnamese got in touch with his manhood. The pilot, he
alleged, gave him thumbs-up as he pushed the dead Vietnamese
out. The next night Rowe bumped into the same gunner at the
same club. He told Rowe not to believe anything he'd said the
night before, that it was all bullshit. Rowe told him he had a girl-
friend named Betty who was the best-looking gal in Las Vegas.
The gunner nodded and turned to his beer, as if to say he de-
tected bullshit.

At dusk a rangy buck sergeant named Belcher approached Rowe
outside the billets. He was tall and blade-thin with gray eyes.

"You Hobbes?"

"Yes, Sergeant," Rowe said.

He looked Rowe over and said, "Belcher, just Belcher."

"Okay."

He told Rowe to grab his gear and follow. The unit, he explained, was out in the boonies most of the time. At present they
were on stand-down, but this was its last night. They were heading out to a new area of operation. As they neared the squad tent,
Belcher said, "We lost Humby and Naider. Guys won't talk much
for a while. Don't push. They're okay."

An NCO in Charm School had warned how new fucking guys,
called NFGs, were treated at first, how grunts often felt like a new
guy was in some way connected to the death of a buddy, or just
plain bad luck. No logic—but this was 'Nam.

Belcher spread the tent flap. A naked overhead bulb dangled

from a tent post. Three bare-chested men played cards on a cot. They glanced up briefly, then returned to the game. They were all frame and wire, no casing—field-hardened—and they glistened with sweat.

"This is Hobbes," Belcher said.

They appeared unimpressed. They were supposed to number eleven, but they were just seven, and Rowe was the seventh. He got a nod or grunt as Belcher named off the squad. The fire team leader was Rains, a blade-thin spec four whose smooth black skin seemed to have a gloss on it. Then there were Leonards, known as C's for his love of C-rations, another black soldier; the white kids, Apple and Johnson; and Paez, a small Mexican American with dark almond eyes and eyelashes a Hollywood starlet would envy.

Paez swung his feet down onto the pallet. "Well, welcome to III-Corps, vacation spot of the tropics. Free tan, free food, free lodgings, and all the exercise a man could want."

C's reached under his cot without sitting up, pulled out an M-60 and rested its stock against the edge of the cot. "Big son-ofabitch like him oughta carry the pig," he said to Belcher. "You said next man comes gets it."

Belcher handed the weapon to Rowe. "You're our man. Get a crib. We're goin' out tomorrow."

Paez smiled, and Rowe did the same only because Paez had. Rowe spread his poncho liner, lay down on the cot next to Paez and pulled the mosquito net closed. Paez lay on his side, his head resting in his hand.

"Where you from?" he asked.

"Las Vegas," Rowe said.

"New Mexico?"

"No, the real one."

"Ah." He turned his back to Rowe and muttered, "He's too damn big to go into tunnels."

"Paez," Rains said. "It's in your blood."

"Time to dream," Paez said.

The card game folded and the men fell silent as they packed and loaded rounds into magazines in preparation for the coming day. Rowe looked about, snatching glances of them cleaning rifles or writing letters in the glow of the bare bulb.

Once the light was snapped off, they drifted to sleep, a sleep best likened to anesthesia. The 155 fired. Rowe lay awake listening to it and thinking of Betty, remembering her naked to the waist, leaning back, her arms supporting her as she looked up, her breasts firm, nipples erect. He wanted badly to masturbate but didn't dare.

He awoke scared and looked about in the dark. The tent walls rippled in a slight breeze, but inside the atmosphere was thick. Snoring flooded the room, and sweaty animal smells dominated the close air. Rowe lay staring at a crease in the tent, wondering if he would ever again sleep well.

They bent under the swirling props of a Huey. Belcher, face painted black and green, told Rowe to clear the chopper as soon as they hit the LZ, especially if it was hot, no dogging it. The M-60, the pig, was their lifeline and Rowe carried it. Belcher patted Rowe's helmet and swung into the seat to his right. Then they were hanging in a cloudless sky above a Kelly-green quilt of rice paddies and berms, a work of cubism, streams and hedgerows and red-clay roads that crisscrossed.

Paez, loaded down with bandoliers of 7.62 mm rounds, plus ammo for his own weapon, sat to Rowe's left. He smiled. Rowe smiled back.

"What you smiling at, meat?" he shouted.

The noise of the whirling blades sucked up words.

"Nothing!" Rowe said.

Paez removed his helmet and took a picture out of the liner, one of a girl with long black hair and big dark eyes. She was holding a cat and waving. "My girl!" he shouted.

Rowe said his girl was named Betty. It seemed important to

have one. Paez motioned to say he couldn't hear. Rowe hollered that Paez's girl was "pretty." Paez put the picture away.

Below, flanked by towns and villages with names like Trang Bang and Chau Thanh and Ben Cua, the most perilous stretch of road in the world, Highway 1, spanned north and south. To the west flowed the Vam Co Dong River, and on the east the Saigon snaked to the fertile delta. Farther east lay the Ia Drang Valley. Rowe saw for the first time Nui Ba Dan, Black Virgin Mountain, at the verge of the Cambodian border, its peak enshrouded by clouds. It seemed something concocted to fit a fairy tale.

The squad was too preoccupied to take notice. They'd seen too much of it up close to show interest. The door gunner locked his fist on his m-60 and leveled the barrel during the descent. As the ground rushed up, minute details grew to exaggerated proportions like a slide brought into focus under a microscope. Before Rowe expected it, the chopper rotated right and hovered about two feet off the ground.

Like crabs at low tide, they scrambled chaotically. Rowe followed Belcher through ankle-deep muck. He half hoped to take fire, just to get it over with, a desire that passed soon enough. He caught his toe on a rock, tripped but kept his footing with Paez's help. "Do that often?" Paez asked.

They set up on a berm, and Rowe locked the butt of the pig into his shoulder. Except for scattered tufts of grass and mud pools, the field was sun-hardened clay. Flies swarmed everywhere. Rowe sweated in places he'd never before sweated in, sweated until he couldn't see. His ears were wet. He wondered just what the hell he'd gotten himself into.

Sergeants ordered them to dig in and establish fire lanes. They alighted like claim-jumpers, elbowing into position for the best views, seizing a spot of red clay as if snatching property with a lakefront view.

Paez stripped to the waist, grinned, then jabbed the blade of his entrenching tool into the clay. When Rowe slipped off his shirt, Paez said he was too white for the sun. Rowe muttered, tossed the shirt aside, and picked up his tool to dig. They worked silently, shoveling dirt into sandbags, which they stacked around the edge to form a parapet as the hole grew.

Breaking the silence, Rowe asked, "Why'd you end up with me?"

Paez shielded his eyes and looked up at the sun. "Gloria."

"Your girl?"

"My charm. I figure Charley's going to kill someone, and it'll be you, not me."

"That makes no sense."

"Look around, meat. Nothing here makes sense. But I figure you're what? Eight inches taller, fifty pounds heavier? A good shield. Besides no one in the squad wants anything to do with an NFG."

Rowe nodded, wiped the sweat off his forehead, and stooped to dig.

They continued digging. From time to time, Paez stopped to measure himself against the wall, and when the parapet was tall enough that all but his shoulders and head were concealed, he tossed his entrenching tool over the sandbags and climbed out.

"Hey," Rowe said, "we've got another eight inches to dig."

Paez lit a cigarette and exhaled. "Hole's fine with me. You've got four inches to dig, meat. And four inches of sandbag to fill." He smiled, drew on the cigarette, and gazed off at Nui Ba Dan.

Shaking his head, Rowe bent over and plunged his entrenching tool into the clay.

A platoon of engineers came in with the next wave of choppers and encircled the camp with concertina. The air was still and hot, but the troops kept at their tasks. There was no respite from the sun until holes were dug. Before the engineers finished stringing the last of three aprons of wire, the company had dug in, and one at a time tent halves and ponchos blossomed above the foxholes. The camp looked like a landfill covered with olive-green rags.

Paez and Rowe, legs dangling over loosely, sat on the parapet. "You got a girl, Hobbes?" Paez asked.

Rowe started to say yes, but let that lie go. "No."

Paez considered this and said, "You look like the kind who gets dumped."

Rowe looked at the hole. "Hole looks pretty lame if you ask me."

Paez said, "I've been in tunnels a quarter that size." He said it took a special mind to appreciate tunneling, that before being drafted he'd studied mining engineering at the University of Texas, El Paso, which, in part, accounted for his interest in tunnels. He described them as small engineering marvels and said no one could possibly understand his interest, especially someone obviously stupid enough to carry an M-60.

Rowe nodded. He thought Paez was a bit too brash for a man so small. Then he recalled the helicopter crewman whom he'd met at the club in Cu Chi, the one who'd been so unabashed one minute when he claimed to have shot Vietnamese soldiers, then so contrite the next as he denied it. Paez seemed far too brash. Rowe looked about and wondered what transformed men like Paez into swaggering pretenders, wondered how he himself would change and how soon change would come. Rowe fumbled in his pocket for some gum.

"You're stupid enough to hang around me," he said.

"Ah," Paez answered and let the conversation die there.

Choppers from Cu Chi landed hot food and free beer. Mess kits suspended by their thighs, the men formed a chow line. Paez kidded with others and ignored Rowe, who by listening learned that Apple was from West Virginia and had been drafted by the Cleveland Indians his senior year in high school and drafted by the Army after playing one season in the minors, that Johnson was from Montana and had never been out of the state until the Army claimed him, that Rains was deeply religious, and Leonards equally superstitious.

Forks scraping their aluminum pans, the two of them sat on

their helmets and ate beef stew, creamed spinach, and pasty peach cobbler cooked from canned peaches.

To make conversation Rowe asked about Paez's girl. Paez swallowed. "Since you brought it up, I'll marry her and raise a dozen kids." He aimed his fork and glanced about. "When I get out of this fucking place."

Rowe took a bite and stared off.

"I know what you're thinking," Paez said. " 'Does Paez always talk like this?' I get on people's nerves."

Cox, the platoon sergeant, came around with a second ration of beer. "Get your smoking done now," he said.

"Sarge, the *Stars and Stripes*. Does the Army expect us to live without scores?" Paez asked.

"Paez, does the Army ever forget the *Stars and Stripes*?"

"Could be. The mail's sometimes a little lost."

Cox asked if Rowe was getting along okay. Paez answered for him, saying he was fine.

"What next?" Rowe asked when Cox had left.

"Nothing, and a lot of it. Get used to it, meat."

"Name's Rowe."

Paez shrugged and looked west where the sun bled into the horizon and a halo of red capped the tip of Nui Ba Dan. He nodded, something feral lurking in his eyes. He swallowed his beer, crushed the can on his helmet, and said in a near-whisper, "Civilization underground, hospitals, fueling stations, whorehouses. I am not a little crazy."

That night Rowe slept fitfully, partly from fear, mostly from sunburn and visions of Betty. He thought to write her a letter saying she'd ruined two lives. In the morning he reconsidered that idea.

The fire base was in Tay Ninh Province east of War Zone C, fourteen klicks from the Cambodian border. It was the dry season and hot. A shovelful at a time, holes expanded into bunkers connected by intricate trenches linked like lacework. Dust abounded, a fine, choking dust that hung over the camp. It infiltrated their pores, their noses and lungs; it pursued them into their sleep and greeted them at dawn.

Boom-boom girls from nearby villages posed around the perimeter, ready to trade themselves for money or cigarettes, all the while charting the company's defenses. Dressed in colorful silk, they looked delicate at a distance but up close were sun-darkened country girls with brown teeth that showed when they giggled. It wouldn't have mattered to the soldiers if the boom-boom ladies had carried spiked clubs and looked like Russian potato farmers. Johnson expressed the prevailing opinion when he said, "It's hard to find red-blooded American gals willing to do the same." Lonely and hyper-hormoned, the soldiers sought comfort and sex. If one wanted a girl, he went over the berm with a VC boom-boom girl, but took rifle and buddies along to stand guard, for in Tay Ninh Province everyone not American was VC.

Idle moments led to talk about home, shared experiences, growing up, girlfriends. It was talk that made Rowe long for home. He never mentioned Betty. When talk made him lonely enough, he went to the berm, where he fantasized that she was the brown-toothed woman under him. When finished, he felt a terrible sense of shame. He didn't want to feel that way but did. He'd say no more indulging. But what else was there?

He tried writing letters, but knowing that some REMF clerk would be reading the words inhibited him. So he wrote the mundane, and everything sounded plastic. He'd write a letter and tear it up. He decided on a log, passed time jotting down observations, thinking someday it would come in handy.

"Five shovelfuls of clay fills one sandbag. The tip of Nui Ba Dan is often circled by doughnut clouds. Belcher must masturbate at night or he can't sleep. Paez wakes up whenever he snores. The sound of bombs dumped by a B-52 on the far side of the mountain reaches us four seconds after the initial blast."

He stored the journal in his backpack and allowed no one to see it.

When they came out of the rubber plantation, they realized it was a bad spot. Open paddies spread before them, and there was no cover. Leonards spat on his hands for luck. The platoon formed a column and moved out. On point some twenty-five paces ahead was Elsworth from the Fourth Squad. Belcher advanced, then Paez. Fifteen feet behind, Rowe carried the M-60.

Elsworth's trousers were black from wading through the rice fields. His jaw had a three-day stubble, and his eyes a nine-month hunger. He knew signs and could smell and hear like an animal. He motioned for the platoon to stop and climbed the berm of a paddy to see the other side. Atop it, he crouched, his head swiveling, nose turned up as if sniffing the wind. He motioned that it was okay.

As they stood, Paez muttered something that distracted Rowe. Then, hard and sudden as an unexpected uppercut, an invisible force knocked Elsworth off the dike. A distinct pop came from the far wood line. The platoon belly-dived to the ground. Shaking, Rowe jammed the butt of the pig into his shoulder.

Paez crawled over. "Welcome to the show, meat."

They fished Elsworth out of the shallow water, zipped him into a body bag, and secured an LZ for a dust off. The chopper came, Elsworth went out, and the platoon started all over as if Elsworth's death had been nothing but an interruption. Paez winked at Rowe as he stood. A spotter plane hovered overhead, the pilot ready to call in an air strike on the sniper, who according to Paez was taking R&R in Cambodia by now.

It was Pham Cua on some maps, Bui Cua on others, a village, nothing, seven huts, a dozen women and children, brown-spotted chickens bobbing heads, the smell of Vietnam all over it. The squad had called on Pham Cua before, seen the inviolable expressions on the villagers' faces, stares that communicated scorn. They searched huts for caches, found nothing, and left, taking a well-worn trail to the west. At a rocky clearing overlooking the rice paddies, Belcher raised a hand. "Smoke 'em if you got 'em," he said as he knelt down and clamped his own lips on a cigarette.

The men scattered among the boulders, all but Paez, who was taking in the sights. Happy to unload it, Rowe lowered the m-60 and propped it against a boulder. He'd lugged it too long already. It was a sweat-maker, a ball-buster, a cross, and he had yet to fire it. Diaphanous thermals shimmered where the sun bore down on the emerald paddies in the lowlands, and the glassy pools mirrored the blue sky and the scattered clouds that floated overhead. To the west the verdant land spooled into rocky hills where the vegetation congealed into a dark-green curtain too intense for the intellect to grasp. It was fairy-tale land.

"Find a rock, Paez," Belcher said.

Paez turned ninety degrees and framed a picture with his hands, a cigarette dangling from his lips. "Wish I had a camera."

"Goddamn it, Paez," Belcher said.

Apple stood to shrug out of the straps that held the radio. The round, sounding more like a ping than a shot, struck the prc-25 and slammed Apple to the ground. Belcher shouted at Paez to get down, but as if deaf, Paez held the cigarette to his lips and gazed nonchalantly at the woods.

A second shot whistled off a boulder, but Paez didn't move, just kept smoking until a third sprayed dust near his feet. Then he pointed his finger where the jungle tapered to a crest. Taking a final draw, he flipped the cigarette aside and headed toward the woods, strolling like a sightseer.

"He on drugs, Hobbes?" Rains asked.

"Just crazy," Rowe said.

Belcher hollered for Apple to get a spotter plane up. Apple shouted that the sniper had killed the radio.

"Tell the goddamn world," Belcher said.

Paez pointed to his crotch. "Hit this, you slit-eyed mother-fucker," he said, raised his middle finger to the sniper and began singing "La Cucaracha."

"Get 'im, Paez!" Leonards shouted.

Belcher ordered full rock 'n' and roll. The squad unloaded on the woods for thirty seconds, pulverized leaves and branches, chiseled stone and chewed roots and scattered nearby animal life halfway to Thailand, after which the quiet that followed seemed holy. Paez walked back, flopped down behind a rock, and lit another cigarette. Closing his eyes, he took a long, deep draw. Belcher grabbed him by the collar and lifted him to his feet.

"Can't a guy just enjoy a damned smoke?" Paez asked. "I mean, can't he without someone trying to shoot him or someone yanking him by the collar?"

The sniper fired another round just to let them know.

Rowe was reading *The Pastures of Heaven*. Paez slouched down and peered at the open pages. He asked if the book was any good. Rowe nodded. Paez claimed Steinbeck was a liberal of convenience, not to be placed on a pedestal.

"Why care?" Rowe asked.

"I don't."

"You're not getting this one," Rowe said.

"Don't want it."

Rowe had to hide books or they disappeared. "Yes, you do."

"Dos Passos," Paez said. "There's a writer with his fingers on the pulse. He'd tell us to throw down our arms and walk away."

"So?"

"So, Steinbeck's a fucking hawk."

"So are we."

"Who's Betty?" Paez asked. "You talk in your sleep."

"A cartoon," Rowe said. "What would Dos Passos say about tunnels?"

Paez winked. "Look for the light at the other end. All will lead to Rome. Some shit like that."

A Chicom 7.63 ripped a perfect round hole in Johnson's helmet, and until the medic removed it, no one could tell he'd been hit. Simpson, a new guy, walked two steps away and puked in a rice paddy. Later they swept a village where the indigies looked at the soldiers as if they knew all about Johnson, where he'd come from, the color of his mother's hair, every detail including the name of the doctor who gave him his first swat.

Monks, a guy in the First Squad who hung with Johnson, lifted up an old man's chin and said, "Nice day. How'd you like your old dick shot off?" His eyes puffed full of hate, he stuffed the sight blade down the front of the *ong*'s pajama bottoms and stared. But the old man didn't seem to care one way or the other.

Belcher sat on a log and propped up his leg, making himself comfortable. He lit a cigarette. He told Monks to make sure the M-16 wasn't on full auto because it would make a terrible mess, then he blew a stream of smoke up at the sky. He puffed on his cigarette and dreamed of fields of corn and pumpkins in October, or whatever, on such occasions, went through the mind of a Kansas farm boy.

Monks flicked the selector switch. He intended to emasculate the old man, and no one in the platoon moved to prevent it, until a kid named Benjamin laid a hand on his shoulder and said, "Be easy, be sound, man. Ain't worth it. Come on, now, think about what your mama would think if you was to harm this ol' fella."

Benjamin was right—it wasn't worth it. The platoon took body count, the Viet Cong kept score.

As he drew away, Monks stared over his shoulder at the old man. "Got 'vc' goddamn tattooed on his ass. I know," he said. "Hell, we all know." He ran a thumb up and down the barrel of his M-16, shouting that he'd remember that old man, that one day he'd see him again.

Belcher finished his smoke and ordered the squad to search. They'd dumped over baskets and were bayoneting piles of straw when the rest of the platoon appeared. The lieutenant ordered them out, claimed the indigies were friendly. Rowe wondered how the hell he knew. Was it indexed on the map?

About half a klick from the village a group of boys, the oldest probably ten, greeted them. The soldiers craved anything American, especially the mundane—hamburgers, hot showers, ice cream, a girl in tight jeans, the smell of a new-mown lawn. Here they settled for kids with irresistible grinning faces vending oversweet soft drinks and tasteless rice cakes. "Hey, Joe, numba one sweet, same, same, boom boom. You buy." Kids being one of their weaknesses, they bought soft drinks and sweets.

Rowe gazed at Nui Ba Dan, its peak ringed in clouds. He thought of the clouded peaks of the bitterroots, and of Betty and summer in Montana—a night when he'd heard the splash as she urinated in the bathroom, and he'd reached over and had run his hand up and down the sheet where she'd lain. It was warm and smelled of her. Intimate, wonderful.

Rain pelted the ground and puddled on the floor of the bunker. While the monsoon drummed outside, they sat cross-legged on cots and passed the pipe around. Apple handed it to Paez, who took a long, languorous hit and held the smoke deep in his lungs. He passed the pipe to Rowe. Rowe took a hit and passed it on.

Everything was damp, the whole camp a mound of mold. Mildew formed on T-shirts overnight. The fire base was a huge fungus. Some acrimonious grunt had named it Green Acres, which became its designation and was decidedly appropriate. They hung a sign that read WELCOME TO GREEN ACRES, HOME OF THE JOLLY GREEN GIANT AND A FEW UGLY ELVES.

"How come you got no more picture of Gloria, Paez?" Apple asked.

Paez, who'd lost the picture in a tunnel, exhaled and leaned back, letting the drug take him. "Got her up here," he said, pointing to his head.

"Probably the only place she's ever been."

Paez gave Apple a glassy-eyed look. "Don't mess with her. Fuck with my food or water. Gloria's off-limits."

Rowe took another hit and passed the pipe.

"Yeah, leave the man alone, Apple," Rains said. "Man's girl's sacred. Scripture say a man and woman be each other's temple."

Apple's face glowed like a white moon in the thin light of the gas lantern. "Here we go. The Bible. What's it say about the goddamn monsoon? Tell us a story."

Besides the days that rolled one into the next and the everpresent sight of Nui Ba Dan, continuity existed mostly in their stories. C's had ordered a travel guide to the best inns in Europe and read the itinerary as if leaving the next week; Apple got drunk one night, fell into a foxhole, and slept through a mortar barrage; Belcher had fished a river with a hand grenade.

"Got no story."

The pipe went the circuit again. As Apple reloaded it from his stash, he asked what day of the week it was. No one seemed quite sure. It wasn't a Friday or Saturday and not a Sunday, for Rains would know. They settled on Tuesday. Apple puffed off the pipe and nudged Belcher's forearm.

Apple coughed out the smoke. "Where were we? Days?"

"Hobbes knows," Belcher said. "He keeps track of every shit he takes. Puts it in his journal. Thing's thicker 'an a . . ." He gazed at Rowe, his eyes dope-thick, and asked him what it was thicker than.

"Thicker than the bullshit in here," Rowe said.

They measured days by casualties, for they were operating above the plantation lands. The days had been mostly lucky days after Johnson's death. Near Chau Thanh the company had lost three on an operation with an ARVN battalion because the Vietnamese didn't block the retreating VC, and the platoon lost two on a sweep through a village east of Black Virgin Mountain. But Rowe's squad was charmed.

Pages in his journal had become frayed and fat, the cover warped. He recorded what he could, though every event seemed part of a continuum—the same villages, same trails in a palling cycle—and wherever they went, if there were holes, Paez checked them out. Any progress in the war had little effect on them. At least they couldn't tell any difference. Body count didn't matter. A dozen, a hundred, two hundred dead didn't stop the war, didn't slow it, and the only territory they rightfully claimed was in front of their sight blades. They held what they held because of fire-power. This was absolute. The platoon could dispense as much havoc as one of Genghis Khan's entire armies, but all that did was keep some of them alive to the next day.

Paez passed on the pipe, as did Rains. Leonards, who'd been silent, sat holding the pipe in his lap. He said he needed a new charm. His were wearing out. Water trickled down the sandbag wall behind his head.

"Take Rowe," Paez said. "He dropped out of school, ran away and joined the Army. Talks about a girl in his sleep, but won't talk about her to his best friend. Man's memories are sacred."

The pipe went out as it came to Apple. He leaned near the lantern as he lit it, his face contoured in flickering shadows. "Thick as bullshit," he said.

"We shouldn't get high. It's unmilitary," Belcher said.

"What's that have to do with Gloria?" Apple asked.

Belcher shook his head. "Who's Gloria?"

"You ever saw her, you'd go crazy," Paez said. A drip of water splattered on his nose. He stared at the leak. "Are we sick of rain? Why're you so damn quiet?" he asked Rowe.

Rowe shrugged. He was thinking about being dry, being in the dry heat of the Mojave, a mild autumn, red-rocked rims and sparse vegetation. He remembered a letter he'd written home, a short, cautious fabrication saying he was in a safe place, that he'd landed a job as a clerk and spent most of the time reading. He'd asked for books, paperbacks, and ointment for athlete's foot. He hoped they'd come.

"I got books coming," he announced.

"You heard 'bout Noah and the Ark. 'At's more rain 'an we'd ever see," Rains said.

"What's Noah got to do with anything?" Paez asked.

"Man can't complain's all. Bunch of sinners. An' books don' make you no less'a one."

Paez put on his helmet to block the drip. "You know, Rains, we said no religion. Who's hogging the pipe?"

"Know what I think?" Apple asked and passed the pipe.

Paez sucked on the dead pipe. "Needs a reload, Belcher," he said, then to Apple, "What do you think?"

"This sounds like a bunch of fucked-up dope talk."

They bent over laughing.

When the laughter died, C's coughed and leaned back. "Man, I been thinkin'. You know, thinkin' serious."

"Sure you have," Apple said.

"Hey, man, I'm serious. I don't wanna go home no freak. Don't wanna be no armless or legless man everybody stare at. I mean, anything but that. You guys is my pals. Don't let me go home no freak." He touched an index finger to his temple.

It was as if a whistle calling for silence had been blown. They sat unmoving as the rain beat down and C's looked from man to man. Then his eyes settled on Rains, who said, "Don't look at me."

"Dope talk," Apple said. "Crazy goddamn dope talk."

"Dope talk," Paez said.

Belcher packed the pipe with hash. As he leaned to pass it to Paez, a mortar round exploded. Rains doused the lantern, and Paez missed the handoff. As the pipe splashed into ankle-deep water, he shouted, "Shit! We'll never find it."

"Charley's got no respect for a man. I mean, what's sacred?" Apple said.

"A-fucking-men," Paez said.

Another mortar round hit the camp.

"Let's get," Belcher said as a third exploded, this one closer.

"Shee-it," Apple said.

They headed into the rain-soaked trenches. Stumbling and sliding in mud, Rowe asked why Paez told the squad about him talking in his sleep.

"Don't you just love the rain?" Paez answered. "It purifies the world, don't you think?"

The fire had come from an area infested with tunnels, so they rounded up the villagers. Noticeably absent were young men, as if some singular pestilence had descended on the country and claimed every living male between the ages of sixteen and fifty. Belcher radioed the fire base to say they had command of fifty indigenous personnel, whom they called "gooks" or "slopes" or "indigies," for it was easier to herd indigies out of their homes and then torch their huts than to make humans suffer.

The indigies gazed at them with patient expressions, the kind that long-suffering people possess. They compliantly moved into a clearing, took the offered cigarettes and squatted down. Young women nursed their infants, old *Ba*s chewed betel nut, old men smoked. They'd seen conquerors—the Japanese, the French—knew what was required.

Apple used his Zippo to light the skirt of a thatched roof. Division had a policy against torching huts, but there were no generals in the field. They dumped incendiaries inside the huts, and the villagers watched their homes consumed in orange flame. In 'Nam fire seemed to burn hotter and smoke turn blacker. The villagers stared into the flames, waiting now for the platoon to leave so they could pack up what little they had and carry it to a relocation center.

Leonards said the squad was "pissin' off the get-even god." Belcher shrugged. Rowe figured it was hard to find a moral high ground. The smell of charred straw and wood drifted from the village. They found a tunnel. Shedding backpack and bandoliers, Paez pulled out a flashlight and took the lieutenant's .45. He tied himself to the rope, raised both his arms, and squirmed into the opening.

As the men smoked, Rains fed out line. From time to time he tugged on it. Peaz had been down fifteen minutes. Then Rains had no more rope to feed and found it had gone slack. Belcher removed his helmet and sat down by the hole. The lieutenant said to give the line a tug. Rains wrapped the rope around his wrist and reeled it in. The squad crowded around, peering down as he gathered in rope an arm length at a time until the running end hung over the opening. Paez had untied.

"Call him up," the lieutenant said.

Belcher squatted over the hole, cupped his hands to his mouth, and pausing in between, hollered Paez's name three times. "Maybe he's lost." Still looking down the hole, Belcher stood up.

The lieutenant said they could borrow Simmons from another platoon to go down and take a look-see.

"He'll come out," Belcher said.

"I'll go down," C's said.

The lieutenant shook his head. "Ten minutes, then we get Simmons."

Belcher reluctantly agreed, and gave another call.

"What's all the shouting?" Paez stood next to Apple, who hadn't taken notice.

"Where the hell'd you go?" the lieutenant demanded.

"Short rope, long tunnel, sir," Paez said and added that he'd come up where a papa *san* was staring him in the eye like he was expected. "I shook his hand and wished him a nice vc day," Paez said.

The lieutenant said, "Blow the hole. And goddamn it, Paez, you don't fucking untie, got it?"

As they plodded through the entrance to Green Acres, Paez

said, "There's one that runs to Hanoi and back to Saigon. We just haven't found it."

The kill zone looked like something cooked to a lumpy paste and dumped on a plate to spoil—flies everywhere. Paez crossed himself and kissed his fingers.

"I thought you didn't believe," Rowe said.

"I don't," Paez said.

Medics issued stretchers and body bags and handed out a balm to apply to nostrils and advice—wear bandanas and watch for unexploded rounds while digging for bodies. Rowe stepped out and immediately sank to his ankles. Flies blitzed about so thick the men could reach out and grab a handful. Some walked away to puke.

Paez told Rowe to grab a pair of legs. They turned the body over to lay him face up and zip him in a bag. It was like lifting a barrel of water. At the count of three they hoisted him onto the stretcher, then grabbed the handles and picked up the load. They heard a moan and quickly unloaded the stretcher.

The body rolled back into the hole, where it lay motionless, its blank face seemingly indignant, but very dead. Paez noticed dirt shifting beside the body and dove down on hands and knees, digging furiously with both hands, pitching fountains of loose dirt up in the air. Rowe shouted for a medic, then joined Paez, tearing at the ground with bare hands.

When they unearthed the vc, Rowe held his wrist and found a pulse, weak, but a pulse nonetheless. He dripped canteen water on the man's eyelids and gently wiped away dirt until the eyelids fluttered. The vc blinked his eyes open, then seeing Rowe, gasped and began to squirm. "He's alive," Paez said. "Imagine!" He told him to take it easy, that a doctor was coming, and soon a medic was cutting away the uniform with surgical scissors.

The medic studied the wounds.

"How bad, Doc?" Paez asked.

"Shrapnel," the medic said, "in the upper back." He probed

around. The VC didn't exhibit pain, though he had to be feeling it. "And a piece . . . near the spine." His hands sure and quick, the medic started an IV and cleaned their man—for by then he was theirs. He bandaged the wounds and shot morphine into the feeder tube. He said he'd call a dust off ASAP and told them to cart the man to the helipad.

Apple and C's peered down. Like Lazarus, the VC had been to the other side, and his eyes told the tale. Smiling, Paez said, "Bet it's hardly the heaven you anticipated."

"You the luckiest fucker in 'Nam," C's said.

Word of the miracle spread. A modest crowd of curious grunts gathered to watch as they hoisted their man onto the stretcher. They toted him to the LZ, where they guarded him jealously as others came to have a look-see. Some reached down to shake his hand. Others touched him gently or stuck packs of cigarettes or chewing gum on the stretcher beside him. One scratched initials on a bullet and put it in the man's hand. Others simply looked and shook their heads. Awe on every face.

The lieutenant hung around after his peek. "Don't you two think he'll be okay?"

"Sir?" Paez asked.

"Do you have to . . . ? I mean."

"Sir, we pulled him out," Paez said. He held a lighted cigarette up to Lucky's mouth.

The lieutenant nodded. "So you did. Carry on."

They took turns keeping his lips moist with canteen water and holding cigarettes for him while he smoked. As they lifted him onto the helicopter, he looked up and said, "*Chet roi*," meaning "dead."

They tried to nap, which was difficult. The heat was despotic, and by then the odor had permeated everything. Paez wrote to Gloria, telling her what a beautiful day it was and how he'd made a friend. He read the letter aloud. Rowe asked how he could lie like that.

"It's what she wants to hear. If you had a girl, you'd know."

Two Chinooks landed. Out of their bellies came two bull-dozers followed by a unit of combat engineers, who donned masks and went to work. The company sat atop bunkers and watched the bulldozers scuttle back and forth, puffing spouts of diesel smoke and plowing with tireless energy as if there weren't enough dirt in Vietnam for them to move. Methodically, they rent a hole wide enough and deep enough to accommodate the dead.

The pit finished, the operators turned their machines to the bodies, after which three medics poured gas over the remains. A sergeant pulled the pin on an incendiary, looked away from the mass grave, and tossed the grenade. A wall of orange burst from the pit. Sitting more than a hundred yards away, the squad felt the heat as the sky blackened. When the fire died, the bulldozers plowed again, and the flies swarmed the camp. Paez said Green Acres was a perfect name for a cemetery.

Battalion helicoptered in hot food, beer on ice and a movie, *The Sound of Music,* along with a dispatch heralding the company. The men filled their trays but picked at the food. Rains stared at the mound, muttering, about what Rowe couldn't tell. Belcher lit a joint and passed it, and Rains, who never smoked dope in his life, took a draw.

"*The Sound of Music?*" Apple said. "Who the fuck's in charge of this war? I mean, really."

In his journal Rowe wrote, "Today the captain said we killed seventy-two but didn't mention the one we saved whose name was probably Nguyen; they're all named Nguyen. He smoked too much. Paez lied to Gloria. Rains lost God." Rowe had so many stories. He thought of whom he'd want to hear them. Grady? Maybe. Betty? Then soft in his head, "Betty."

A kid named Newman came back from R&R. Somehow he had ended up in Hawaii by mistake. He'd met a nurse, he said, and

shacked up with her for four days. He walked around letting anyone who wanted to sniff his fingers, claimed it was the smell of
round-eyed pussy, grade-A American. He said he was thinking
about cutting off a finger and preserving it. When he told this to
Rowe's squad, Apple said, "Why don't you cut your dick off and
preserve it?"

"Soreheads. Just jealous. I'm probably the only grunt in the
history of this fucking war who got to Hawaii."

"Cut your dick off anyhow," Belcher said.

Paez set his book down. He was reading Malory's *Tales of King
Arthur*, which he'd picked up from some helicopter pilot in trade
for a Montagnard crossbow. "Guy's full of it," he said.

Rowe looked up from cleaning the M-60. "So."

"I been thinking," Paez said. "We're subterranean by nature.
We long to be inside things. The womb's our first home. A cave.
A blanket's a womb. What's the first thing you want to do with a
woman? Get inside of her, see what's hidden beneath her clothes.
Another cave. The womb again."

"What's the point?"

"The point? There is no fucking point," he said.

"Do you write Gloria about going into tunnels?"

He took a drag off his cigarette and stared off toward Nui
Ba Dan. "That mountain's full of tunnels. Most dug by the Viet
Minh. A regiment could hide in them. Hospitals. Barracks. Service clubs with beer on tap. Health spas. Hotels with maid service. Tile entries. Baths like Romans had. It's a big mountain.
Think of the possibilities." He crushed the cigarette out on a
sandbag and turned to Rowe. "I write her about blue skies and
dumb grunts like Newman." He looked at the mountain, its peak
covered with wispy clouds. "Let's put in for R&R in Hawaii. You,
me, on a beach. Gloria can meet us. Bring one of her cousins,
one of the less fat ones."

"Hawaii? You heard what Newman said." Rowe touched some
oil to the trigger housing.

"He's full of shit."

That afternoon they signed up at the headquarters tent for R&R. Marshall, the company clerk, a draftee from Mendocino, California, said, "Where the officers go?" He was a small man with unmilitary sideburns.

"That's where we want to go," Paez said.

"Officers and senior noncoms. Grunts like you could be an embarrassment."

"An embarrassment? Rowe knows important people. He's got a cousin in Congress. MAC-V wouldn't want an inquiry over R&R, would it?"

"Who's Rowe?"

"Hobbes." Paez aimed an index finger at Rowe. "This guy, my buddy."

Marshall looked Rowe over.

"Don't let his appearance fool you," Paez said. "I've seen pictures of him in a tux at the governor's ball."

Marshall shook his head. "Not likely." He handed over the forms to fill out. "I don't care, but get this straight—you're not going. This is the fucking Army, and the Army doesn't send grunts to Hawaii for R&R."

They were summoned to headquarters to see Lieutenant Bredlau, the company executive officer, who tossed the requests down on the table. Grinning at them, Marshall opened himself a soft drink and downed it in two gulps.

"It's not policy exactly," the lieutenant said, "but enlisted men don't go to Hawaii. Not grunts."

"Sir, they let REMFs go, at least that's what I hear, and they're nothing but butt licks," Paez said.

Bredlau shook his head. "Bangkok. All the whores you'd ever want, Paez."

"Hawaii, sir."

"And you, Hobbes?"

"Hawaii," Rowe said.

"Paez, you think being a tunnel rat gives you license around here?"

"Sir, just the privilege of going down."

"Well, it doesn't."

"How about you, Hobbes? You think you're privileged?"

"Sir, it's enough privilege to serve in a place like Green Acres."

Marshall went into coughing spasms. Lieutenant Bredlau told him to go outside and get some water and said to Rowe, "I'm not laughing." He weighed matters thoughtfully and asked, "What's your cousin's name?"

"Cousin, sir?" Rowe asked.

"The one in Congress."

"He'd rather not say, sir," Paez said.

Lieutenant Bredlau shuffled papers from one side of the table to the other. "I'd rather he say."

"Sir, if it's all the same I promised I wouldn't," but it suddenly occurred to Rowe Hawaii might not be such a fantasy, for Grady knew senators and congressmen. He'd introduced Rowe to more than one on occasions when they'd eaten lunch.

"It's not all the same." With a shrug, Bredlau signed the forms. "Not until March," he said. "And there's a good chance you'll go to Bangkok or Singapore."

Paez winked at him. "Sir, maybe they don't understand what we do."

On their way out Marshall grabbed Rowe's arm. "You really have a cousin in Congress?"

"Would Paez lie?"

Marshall shook his head. "How would I know?"

"You wouldn't," Rowe said, then asked, "Can you get me a call stateside?" Rowe figured Grady might appreciate a ring. Besides, Betty had been in his thoughts. He'd even composed letters to her, which of course he never sent.

"Maybe," Marshall said. "I'm interested in Hawaii."

"Planning on deserting?" Paez asked.

"Put in a request," Rowe said. "I can fix it up."

"Same time as you guys?"

"Sure," Paez said. "Tell the lieutenant you're in, but don't expect one of Gloria's cousins."

They left him asking who Gloria was.

Though they could see barely twenty feet ahead, they scaled Black Virgin Mountain. The trails were steep and slippery. Division had sent handlers with three German shepherds to sniff out the enemy, but a third of the way up the animals began to cough. The mountain was too rough, a handler explained. One dog coughed up pink foam. Its handler stroked it and talked gently, but it died anyhow—pulmonary arrest. The lieutenant sent the other two dogs back.

Not far from where the dogs gave out, they came upon a tunnel, a deep one.

"We can just blow it," the lieutenant said, which was only a formality, as Paez never refused to go down.

Paez looked up at the black sky, then at the lieutenant, and nodded to indicate he'd go. They hadn't eaten, so the lieutenant called for a chow break first and the men opened their Cs. Paez took Rowe's Oreos and Rains's peaches and wolfed them down. Finished, he stripped off his poncho and gear. C's unhooked his tiger's claw from his neck and placed it around Paez's.

"Luck, man," he said.

"Don't untie," the lieutenant ordered.

Rope about his waist, and flashlight and gun in hand, Paez disappeared just as the clouds burst. Rain beat on the forest with a sound as deafening as a waterfall, and water channeled down trails, transforming them into rivers. The mountain seemed alive. The men kept one eye on the trail and one on the tunnel while wishing they had a third to watch the mountain.

They were startled when the rope went slack and Paez popped out of the hole unexpectedly. He scrambled away, shivering, his lips chalk-white. He held the gun, but the flashlight was gone.

He pointed at the opening, said, "Blow it," and stumbled to the side, where he sat down on a boulder and stared at his feet.

Rains and Apple tossed in concussion grenades. The hole, like a gaping mouth, spat out dirt and black smoke as the ground rumbled. The lieutenant ordered them to head down. Only then did Paez look up.

"What'd you see down there?" Belcher asked.

Paez shook his head. "Can't see in the dark."

Paez didn't move. Rowe handed over his gear and helped him to his feet.

They stayed two more days at the base of Nui Ba Dan, and Paez, his smile gone, kept to himself and wouldn't talk. Rains and Apple urged Rowe to find out what had happened, but two attempts earned a mere shrug. As they loaded onto Hueys to return to Green Acres, Paez told the lieutenant that he wasn't going down anymore but refused to say why.

In January they were helicoptered to Cu Chi for a stand-down. Rowe was glad to leave behind Green Acres and the smell of death that never quite dissipated. Though the camp was behind, the reminders of death seemed stronger. C's claimed the field was haunted; few doubted that.

Division billeted C Company near the motor pool, where diesel oil and solvents mixed with the odors of Cu Chi and human sweat made breathing unpalatable. They strung up a net and played volleyball. Rumors circulated—operations north, supposedly in Binh Long or a search and destroy in the Delta or the Iron Triangle. They ignored rumors and smoked dope and drank beer.

It was a sweltering day, too hot to do anything. The walls of the tent were raised to capture whatever gypsy air decided to slip through. Occasionally a breeze informed them that Cu Chi smelled no better than Green Acres. Paez lay on his cot scanning the *Stars and Stripes* as Rowe field-stripped the pig and cleaned it. Paez lit a Lucky Strike. His smile had returned, and though he refused to discuss Nui Ba Dan, he was talking again. He snapped the paper. "The Great Gringo says we're turning the war around."

"You don't say," Rowe said absentmindedly.

"No, I don't. The Prez does. Trouble with gringos is they don't listen. It's straight from his lips. War's all but over. That all right?"

"Doesn't matter."

Paez rolled his legs over the edge of the cot and sat up. "What does?"

"Jock itch," Rowe said. "Athlete's foot, sore arches, rash, leech bites, and a dose if I could find a whore."

"I've been thinking about Lucky," Paez said. "Let's pay a hospital visit and see what happened to him."

"How the hell would they remember one vc?"

Paez drew off his cigarette and used the tip to burn a hole in the photo of Lyndon Johnson. He blew smoke at the ceiling and spread the paper. "An unmanned craft landed on the moon— over two weeks ago. The Great Gringo wants a ten percent surcharge on taxes to lower the budget deficit. He means, of course, to finance the war."

Paez lowered the paper. "We'd win this if they'd hire the Mexican Army. Trouble is, Americans feel too underpaid to get themselves killed. Take a Mexican, he'd gladly go out and get himself killed for this kind of money." He turned to the sports page. "Green Bay beats Oakland. Oakland, where all those antiwar punks smoke dope and get laid." Paez looked over the top of the paper. "You may as well be my wife."

"You don't have one."

"But I will. And you, pathetic gringo, will die old with shriveled balls."

Sergeant Cox, his fatigues black with sweat from hefting the mailbag slung over his shoulder, threw open the flap, looked around, and sniffed.

"What's that smell?" he asked and dropped the bag on a cot.

Rowe said, "The rose of Southeast Asia."

"Hobbes, you're starting to sound like Paez."

Paez tossed the paper aside and asked if he had mail, though there was always mail—his mother, sisters, or Gloria.

Cox said, "Do I bother to look, Paez?" which was what he said to anyone who asked before the mail was handed out.

"Ah, Sarge, you look for sexy parts so you can pound your pud. Everyone knows."

"You're a draftee, aren't you, Paez?" Cox asked.

"Guilty," Paez answered.

Cox shook his head and tossed two letters to Paez. "Be thankful for the war. Peacetime Army wouldn't put up with your shit, Paez."

"I'm very thankful, Sarge."

"Hobbes, you got a letter." Cox, who'd not yet been promoted to sergeant first class, blamed his lack of advancement on Rowe's squad, which he claimed was full of mutinous dope fiends. He flipped an envelope to Rowe, turned the remaining mail over to Paez, and said, "Tell Belcher to get the tent cleaned up."

The envelope, addressed in a flowing cursive, had been taped closed by the censors. Rowe broke the seal. Embossed in bold lettering on white linen paper was an invitation to join in celebration as Betty A. St. James and James A. Norber take vows before God and man, the wedding to take place February 2, 1968, at 7:00 P.M. Enclosed was an R.S.V.P. envelope. Not even Tom! A bead of sweat trickled down Rowe's nose and splattered on the splendid white paper. Folding it in two, Rowe stuffed it in his shirt pocket.

Shouting came from near the motor pool. Rowe walked to the tent flap to see what it was about. Some REMFs were getting up a game of softball. They tossed a ball around, warming up, which seemed ludicrous, as every muscle that needed warming up would be overheated by the time they got around to playing. Rowe asked Paez if he wanted to go watch.

Paez looked up from his letter. "Gloria says she'll meet us. No cousins, but you, her, me in Hawaii, on the beach."

Rowe wondered how Paez would feel if he got a wedding invitation from Gloria. He said grunts didn't go to Hawaii and he could get all the tan he wanted in 'Nam.

"Very cynical. What came in the mail?"

"Nothing. A card." Rowe said he was going to watch the game.

Paez lay back to reread his letter. Rowe stuffed his hands in his pockets and aimed toward the makeshift diamond. The pop of the leather ball in the gloves was a piece of home. A player hollered they were short a man. Rowe shook his head, ambled to the center of the compound, and loitered by the mess hall until he spotted an empty latrine that wasn't burning. He took out the invitation, read it several times, brushed his fingers over the splendid embossed lettering. He held it to his nose and took in the orchid smell, reminiscent of an altar, then he wadded it into a ball, dumped it in the cavity and unbuttoned his fly.

On the morning of January 31, Cu Chi came under mortar attack. Division was near full strength, as most units had been lifted out of the field. Sappers tried to breach the perimeter but failed, this attack followed by more incoming. In the distance, to the south, the battle for Tan Son Nhut erupted, and in the predawn mechanized units were sent out to break the assault on the air base whose outer defenses had been breached.

The next day C Company camped by the helipad, ready to go out. Paez and Rowe sat in harness back to back, napping under ponchos. Belcher informed the squad the whole area of operation was on fire, which seemed pretty self-evident as Division artillery fired outgoing every two or three seconds and naval guns had pelted the corridor between Cu Chi and Tay Ninh relentlessly from dawn to dusk.

At nightfall a strict blackout was enforced, and the company was posted on the perimeter, where Rowe caught random flashes of distant battles. Just before dawn the camp filled with a sense of urgency as the tracks warmed up and helicopters throttled to life. Almost immediately the first of the Hueys lifted off like bees abandoning a hive.

Tracks departed the gate, a harsh grinding of diesel engines marking their passage. Artillery blasted away relentlessly at positions to the south. As the last of the armored personnel carriers rolled out, C Company was ordered back out to the tarmac.

Belcher asked where Paez was, but no one knew. As Rowe's squad lined up behind the Third Squad, Paez came running with his web gear in tow, shouting he had to stop for a piss. It was too dark for Rowe to see clearly, but Paez was smiling, though not his normal smile. As Rowe helped him with his strap, Paez winked and said, "Fuck the Army," which meant much more.

Low clouds hung over the camp. The deep growl of words flowed among them, mixed tones of macho-ness and anxiety. A round-face major called them to attention and said, "Light 'em if you have 'em." A spec four from the Third Squad with SWEET DEATH printed on the back of his flak jacket lit up a reefer. Seeing this, Apple lit up one.

Paez handed Rowe the joint. Rowe passed it on without taking a hit, as did C's. Belcher drew on it and held the smoke in his lungs, then passed it to Rains, who shook his head. More Hueys were landing. Sergeants looked the other way as the weed circulated, even Cox, who walked up and down, telling them for the umpteenth time to check their weapons.

The company lined up to board. Every sound took on inordinate clarity—helicopter blades feathering, metal clattering, boots clopping. Rowe thought to think of something other than what was ahead, and what came to mind was Betty's wedding. He smiled, for this was a great day to attend a wedding.

As they strapped in, Paez asked what was so damned funny. Rowe motioned that he couldn't hear. The Huey shuddered and lurched, then hesitated an instant as if unaware of having breached gravity. It lifted itself smoothly through the light mist, cool, moist air spilling in its open doors. Rowe felt he'd forgotten something and was seized by a momentary panic when he realized it was his journal. He had things to say. How would he remember them?

He asked the door gunner if they could go back for his journal. The gunner pointed to his ears and then the rotating blades and shouted, "Won't be long!" He seemed to want a response, so Rowe nodded and said Wilt Chamberlain was the best.

At two thousand feet the sky cleared. Stars wrapped over the edge of the earth. Save for the sounds of the engine and the whirling blades, it was blissfully silent. The door gunner stared out, face tense, as he aimed his M-60 downward and swung its barrel back and forth.

Over Saigon rocket fire crossed the sky. Passing Hoc Mon the choppers took ground fire, green tracers arching upward gracefully and fading away. A round dinged the side panel and ricocheted off the door gunner's helmet. He looked at Rowe as if to say what luck. Won't be long, Rowe thought.

Crossing Hoc Mon, the craft dipped and circled. Paez was smiling. Rowe shouted for him to give up the goddamn smile. Paez pointed to his ears. Rowe glanced at Rains, whose head was bowed over the barrel of his M-16. The escort ships angled down over a stretch of rice paddies and let go with rockets. C's licked his lips and clutched his tiger's claw, mumbling something. What exactly, Rowe was unsure, but it had to do with dying. The crew chief signaled and the men crouched at the edge of the door.

The craft leveled over a paddy where the air erupted with incoming from AK-47s and Chicom machine guns. C's hesitated. Belcher hollered for him to move, lifted him up and pulled him out. Apple landed first, followed by Paez and Rowe, then Rains and C's and Belcher. Running in the mud was like taking on fifty pounds of added gear.

While a second chopper landed, the first rose, hung suspended as if in doubt of its condition, then burst into flames, disintegrating as it fell. Rowe sank in a hole to his waist. A bullet snapped overhead and inspired him. C's dropped to his knees, cupping both hands over his throat. Rains turned back to help. Paez wheeled about, but Rains shouted for him to go on, shoved C's to the ground and covered him with his own body.

A bullet slapped the dike and spat mud in Rowe's face. He wiped his eyes, notched his finger on the trigger and squeezed. The feel of the stock hammering against his shoulder, the steam and the smoke smoldering from the barrel got blood pumping to his ears. He fired until Paez tapped him on the helmet and told him to stop.

He laid his head on the damp grass and felt the rise and fall of his chest. He thought of Grady's ranch, Montana nights, Betty splayed out beside him, her hair covering the pillow, his hands exploring her, everything new and wonderful. He wanted it to last forever. He could feel her breath as he cupped her cheeks. A warmth filled his belly. Those moments had been God to him. They swallowed his soul. He blinked once and was back on the dike. There was only this, the cool grass, the smell of nitrates, and the cries of wounded asking for help.

They lay listening to helicopters circle and ferry in the rest of the company. Apple said, "They got C's bad." He shouldered his M-79 and pumped a grenade into the brush just to do something with his anger.

Paez leaned toward Rowe. "Don't forget Hawaii," he said, as if to say, "Remember the Alamo."

Belcher threw himself down next to them and asked Paez where his helmet was. Paez touched his bare head.

Cox crawled over to say he was calling in artillery.

"Where's the lieutenant?" Belcher asked.

"*Chet roi.* Him and a bunch, even the company clerk."

Rains dragged C's, who was drowning in his own blood, to the foot of the berm. A medic ran over and applied a compress to the wound, shook his head, said he was sorry. He swooped up his medical kit. Rains aimed his rifle at the medic, told him to come back, that he'd shoot if he didn't. But Rains didn't shoot, and there was no reason for the medic to return.

Rains inched up the slope, where he sat with his back to them, his arms crossed over his knees. "Couldn't say good-bye," he said. "Took his voice box. Is 'at right? I mean, is it?"

The artillery came.

Apple and Rowe tried to pull Rains down, but he pushed them away. Arms folded, he sat the duration of the barrage and remained unharmed, as if C's charms had consigned their power to him. Dust offs landed to pick up casualties. Rains refused to notice Apple and Belcher carrying C's body across the field.

Belcher found a helmet, handed it to Paez, and asked Rains what the hell was going on. Rains said he quit.

"You can't quit," Belcher said.

But Rains said that was the case. He'd stopped, gone on strike, quit the Army. Belcher said to Paez and Rowe, "You didn't hear this," and reached inside an ammo pouch. He pulled out a shot of morphine, which he clenched between his teeth.

Rains asked, "What you doin', man?" and tried to get away, but Belcher grappled him to the ground, jabbed the needle into a thigh and called for another. He gave Rains two more doses and held him until he quit struggling. When it was over, Belcher took a long breath and said, "Keep him close."

At dawn they found themselves in a field of smoldering holes surrounded by fractured earth and splintered trees. The sun rose over the roofs of Hoc Mon and outlined the palm trees, an exotic, postcardlike rendering of paradise, except for the smoke. They heard diesel engines.

Between the company and the shimmering sun a column of APCs churned in slow motion over the charred earth. The nearest ran over a body, which sank into the mud except for one stiff arm.

"Wolfhounds, come on!" a track commander called out.

Rowe's squad followed two APCs through deserted streets lined with skeletal dwellings, paths littered with men, cats, dogs, rats, and pigs, all dead. Rowe wrapped a bandana over his face. Paez asked what day it was. Rowe had no idea. Neither did Belcher or Apple. Nor did Rains, who said he didn't even know how many days they'd been fighting this damned thing. Paez said that's because he was stoned most of the time. Rowe vaguely remembered a variation of this very conversation.

"It's Tuesday or Wednesday," Rowe said. "Or Thursday."

The day didn't matter. They'd been through something. It had been big and terrible. It seemed important to seek some anchor —a day of the week, an outside event, something that marked the moment, so they could look back and know, so they could point to that and say they remembered.

As they advanced on an undefended bridge, the chime of a bell came from behind. It repeated itself—*ca-ching, ca-ching.* Rowe looked over his shoulder. A girl, perhaps fifteen and dressed in white silk, balanced her bicycle and tried to pass the file. Not far behind another followed, and from the same direction a Vespa rode out of the smoldering ruins, its engine hacking like a morning cough.

The girls carried schoolbooks strapped to their backs. They didn't acknowledge the marching soldiers any more than they did the randomly strewn dead or the clouds of black flies or the smoldering craters. The soldiers stepped to the side. The girls passed on with phantom aloofness, seemingly untouched, the sheer white tails of their *áo dàis* sailing behind like pennants as they rode on calmly and purposefully.

His name tag read Digbus. He was a lieutenant in charge of morale—which meant R&R as well. He'd not yet seen a tracer round and had a mama *san* who cleaned his room, and another who polished his boots. He sat behind his desk, shook his head, and told Paez and Rowe to take Bangkok—the best he could do. When Rowe said they'd requested Hawaii months before, he told them Bangkok, Singapore, Kuala Lumpur, and Hong Kong were great, tried to sell the price of whores and booze.

"Sir," Paez said, "we survived Tet. Grunts. See?"

"Whoop-di-fuckin'-do, Paez."

Paez said, "No offense, sir, but I just don't want to go where there's a bunch of dinks, even if the prices are next to free. You understand, don't you?"

"No." The officer stamped their orders for Bangkok and handed over the travel vouchers. As he was also in charge of emergency phone calls, Rowe told him an adopted sister had gotten married and he wanted to congratulate her. The lieutenant, smelling victory, made arrangements for him at the Red Cross.

It took ten minutes to get Grady on the line.

"Rowe, you here?" He sounded amazed to hear from Rowe.

"Grady, you have to say 'over' when you're finished. I'm still in 'Nam, over."

"Hell, boy. We been 'spectin' somethin' terrible."

Rowe explained again that it was necessary to say "over" at the end of a sentence. On a static-filled line they talked small talk for a minute until Grady got used to the idea of saying "over," then Rowe asked for a big favor, fast.

"What you want, Rowe? Over."

"I've got R&R coming and this lieutenant wants to send us to Thailand. Paez, that's my buddy, and I want to go to Hawaii. We asked for Hawaii months ago. Over."

"What's this lieutenant's name? Over."

There was a waiting line of soldiers and Marines. Rowe explained how a call from a senator might influence matters. Grady said he could probably do it. In the corner of his eye Rowe saw the Red Cross lady pointing at her watch.

"I've got to go, Grady."

"I got a job waiting for you, and you forgot to say over."

"Over, Grady."

"Over, Rowe. I'll call them, right now. Over."

"Bye. Over."

"Don't you . . . Hell, Rowe. Good-bye . . . Over."

Pale clouds floated above, the ocean shimmered below. The only enlisted men on the flight, they sat in the last two seats behind

NCOS and officers, many noncombatants who lifted ballpoints and courageously initialed documents. Flight attendants with frosted-pink lips served up cheerful smiles, in-flight meals, and drinks. They placed pillows behind the soldiers' heads and said it was nice to have them aboard. They bent close so the smell of their perfume and the graze of their mint breath would remind the soldiers of all they missed.

Their smiles were something vaguely remembered and made Rowe wish he was meeting Betty in Honolulu. He'd settle for less, though, in truth, he expected nothing. A rosy-cheeked, pony-tailed redhead named Terry made several out-of-the-way trips to their seats. She hung around to ask questions about their comfort—did they want a magazine? another soft drink? She looked at Rowe affably, but Paez commanded her attention. When he looked up with his wet brown eyes and said he'd like a copy of the *Los Angeles Times* editorial page, she shot away. She smiled, handed him an editorial page from the *San Francisco Herald-Examiner,* and said, "I like bright men."

He snapped the paper open, said, "This is more like it," and began reading about Bobby Kennedy announcing his run for the presidency. Rowe looked out the window and watched a ship plow over the ocean; it reminded him of a Monopoly board piece. Terry reappeared to see if Paez was enjoying the paper. She asked where he was from. He told her Texas, and she said, "My favorite state after Hawaii."

"I don't want to go back," he said, and to make things clear added, "except for my girl." He said he was supposed to meet Gloria in Hawaii. Terry said sometimes girls don't show up. He smiled as if remembering a joke and said, "It's nice of you to pay us so much attention."

Rowe said, "Us?"

To be cordial, she asked Rowe's hometown. When he said Las Vegas, she smiled politely and said she was from Vermont, which she described as unlike Las Vegas, beautiful but provincial. As the plane descended for the final approach, she checked their seat belts, then leaned over and handed Paez a note upon which she'd written her name and the hotel where she was registered.

They taxied onto American soil and deplaned to face scenery that looked all too familiar — palm trees, tropical vegetation — no protesters, no signs, just a man with an electronic megaphone shouting instructions and a dozen Hawaiian women in grass skirts waving tiny American flags. When Rowe and Paez stepped onto the ramp, Terry whispered in Paez's ear and kissed his cheek. Rowe got a cordial handshake.

As two women draped leis around the soldiers' necks, three musicians, two with ukuleles and one with a string guitar, accompanied a troop of women who sang and danced a hula. Then the soldiers were hustled onto buses by the man with the megaphone, who also handed out itineraries and tourist guides.

Paez and Rowe were booked into the Hilton Hawaiian Village, where Paez asked the desk clerk for messages. "Nothing for a Mr. Paez," he said and asked about baggage. Paez showed him a carry-on. As he handed over the keys, he told them if they needed anything to visit the shops and charge everything to the room, as Grady St. James was picking up the tab.

"Grady?" Paez asked.

Rowe had mentioned the name, as he had other friends, but had never talked about his relationship with Grady or his wealth. He decided not to start now and settled on saying, "Grady has a little money."

Paez stepped inside the suite and whistled. "This is living," he said. "How much money?" They wandered about touching fabrics and furniture. Paez flipped on the TV, turned down the volume and picked up the telephone. Rowe left him to his conversation and went to the shower, where he lathered up for half an hour under a hot spray and rinsed until his skin wrinkled.

Paez was slumped on the couch watching television with the volume off.

"What's up?" Rowe asked.

He said Gloria was out with friends and he'd talked to her

mother. "She didn't call me Paco," he said. "She's always called me Paco." He shrugged. "Maybe I'm too old for Paco. I need a shower."

After shopping, they dressed in sandals, flower print shirts, and matching shorts that underscored the whiteness of their legs and strolled the beach. They bought hot dogs and Cokes and sat under a cabana. A breeze blew in. Children dug in the sand, and men in dark sunglasses sat and stared at bikini-clad women as surfers paddled out looking for waves. Three teenage boys tossed a football and made diving catches into the gentle breakers. Two small girls, their mother pulling them along, telling them not to bother people, stopped passersby to say hello.

Paez raised his paper cup. "To Hawaii."

Rowe tapped his cup to Paez's. "Hawaii." He started to toast again, to America this time, but a sudden pain hit the back of his skull.

"You okay?" Paez asked and checked Rowe's eyes.

Rowe shook it off. "Fine. Let's walk."

Though he felt dizzy getting up, Rowe was better once he stood. They stepped out of their sandals and carried them so as to let their toes sink into the warm sand. They took in every sight— women, ocean, hotels, surfers staying with fruitless waves. They found an uncrowded spot and sat down near four young women in string bikinis. They sat with their backs to them so as not to perturb them. Rowe just wanted to hear them laugh.

Paez leaned back on his elbows as they stared at the waves. Rowe thought about Betty, which made him feel small and lonely. In time the sweating returned. As it beaded down his forehead, he began to shiver and a transitory pain reeled about the back of his skull. His skin broke out in goose bumps and his ears began to ring. Paez told him his lips were white.

"As white as my legs?"

"I'm serious."

Figuring whatever it was would pass, Rowe insisted he was fine, and the shivering did pass—momentarily. It returned uncontrollably. Paez became a blur. The beach swirled. Rowe pitched forward and threw up. Paez grabbed him and patted his back, encouraged him to stand, but Rowe was too weak to do so.

The young women gathered up their belongings. One said, "Disgusting," as they shook sand from their blanket.

"Animals," another said.

They narrowed their eyes and looked at Rowe. One asked why soldiers didn't show more respect for people.

"My friend's sick," Paez said. "You ever been sick?"

"Soldiers!" the one carrying the blanket said.

They carried their belongings and replanted themselves down the beach, complaining to people nearby. It didn't matter; Rowe couldn't hear anything clearly by then.

Paez laid Rowe's arm over a shoulder and hoisted him up. As they walked by the women, Paez said, "Ever been sick?"

"Drunks!" one hollered.

"Bitches," he muttered as he guided Rowe off the beach.

Paez explained to the house doctor that they were on leave and had only a few days to enjoy, that Rowe was Army property and truly only Army doctors were permitted to malpractice on him, which made the doctor smile. After listening to Rowe's chest and looking down his throat, the doctor wrote a prescription.

"Probably a stomach virus," he said. "I can't be sure without tests. Symptoms match a dozen illnesses, and food poisoning."

"No tests," Rowe whispered.

The doctor shook his head and stood. "I should report this to the health department. He may have something that could infect many people."

Paez smiled. "He hasn't got the clap if that's what you're thinking."

The doctor nodded. "No tests. I hope he feels good enough to enjoy his stay." He looked at Paez. "Keep the room dark and let him sleep. If the fever gets out of control, put him in a tub with ice and run cold water. Call if you need me." He handed over his card and left.

By then the chills were severe. The ceiling whirled as if it were going to fall. A vague outline by the bedside, Paez propped Rowe's head up so he could drink, and later bought hot ox-tail soup—a Hawaiian version of the Jewish mother's chicken broth—to restore him. Rowe awoke from the fog to see Paez dial the phone only to hang up. Another time, though Rowe couldn't tell whether it was in a dream or not, Paez was in a heated conversation and slammed down the receiver. Then later still, Rowe felt a damp cloth on his forehead, and Paez was beside him, assuring him he was doing fine.

Rowe awoke the morning of the third day rejuvenated but parched. Sounds and colors, even the white ceiling seemed to take on an intensity that was too much for his senses. Whatever had hit him was over and had left him with renewed awareness. He called to Paez, who didn't answer. After showering, Rowe went to the living room and sat on the couch, feet propped on the coffee table as "Rhapsody in Blue" played on the radio. He ordered lunch with a bottle of Beaujolais as it sounded good, then opened the curtain and watched sailboats atilt on the bay.

Paez returned at dusk. Rowe was on a second bottle of wine. Paez tossed himself down on the couch and said, "You're better." Rowe asked where he'd been.

Paez held out a clean glass. "Got tired of watching you sleep," he said.

"Gloria?" Rowe poured wine into Paez's glass.

"No Gloria," Paez said and looked pensively at the glass of wine. "Terry."

That said everything. "Oh."

Paez shrugged and stood to turn on the TV. "She helped with you, so I felt obligated to go to the airport."

They downed the bottle and ordered another along with two porterhouses, salads, baked potatoes, and cherries jubilee.

"You asked for Betty," Paez said.

"Grady's daughter. You were right all along. I'm the kind women dump."

"I'm sorry about that. Well, here's to her and Gloria," Paez said and raised his glass.

"To them," Rowe said.

"We'll be needing wine," Paez said.

Rowe ordered two more bottles and tipped the room waiter fifty dollars on Grady's credit. They drank the first bottle, praising the wine's splendid attributes though they had no idea what those qualities were other than alcohol.

"The aftertaste of a Julie Andrews kiss," Paez said.

Rowe grimaced. "The texture of Cornish raspberries."

"Winsome on the palate," Paez said, and they toasted.

They were watching a rerun of a *Beverly Hillbillies* episode when Paez began to wipe his eyes with the back of his hand. With his other, he held his glass for Rowe to fill and stared as if watching the screen. He drank and talked about everything but Gloria. He wiped his damp eyes with the back of his wrist and held the wineglass out.

"I didn't go to the airport because of Terry," he said. "I was going to desert, go home and find Gloria."

"Why didn't you?" Rowe asked.

Paez's eyes seemed as hollow as the hole on Nui Ba Dan, and he looked at Rowe as if he should know, should realize this one thing. Paez had come back because of him. Rowe told him he understood.

"You want to know about Nui Ba Dan?" Paez asked.

Rowe poured wine and Paez explained how he'd crawled around a curve, and suddenly he wasn't alone. He could hear them breathing. One touched him. Then a hand snatched the flashlight and shined it in his eyes. It was, he claimed, like confronting evil. "I thought I was charmed, but I wasn't, was I? I lost it that day, and then . . . her."

Rowe said he was sure Paez was charmed.

It was clear Paez didn't believe it. He said, "No. In the mountain she took the charm from my life."

Rowe suggested they sit on the beach and listen to the surf, but Paez shook his head and went to the balcony, where he stared at the stars. Even when Rowe brought wine and joined him, he kept staring off. Rowe gave him his glass.

"We've got to salute Grady St. James," Rowe said. "Besides you, my only friend."

"To Grady, who got me to Hawaii."

They stayed drunk three days, then flew on another jetliner back to 'Nam.

They were promoted to spec four the day they returned, then the Army separated them, Paez going to a new squad. They stayed in the same platoon under a new platoon sergeant, Mug Tailor, a large, muscular black from Arkansas, and a new platoon leader, James Bull, an ocs second lieutenant from Alabama. The company was operating in Boi Loi Woods.

Rowe had seven months in the boonies; Paez was working on ten — no scratches. It was time to consider mortality, time to think about Cu Chi, burning shit and watching movies. Rowe requested a transfer; Paez volunteered to be a tunnel rat.

Rowe told him he was nuts.

Paez wiped sweat from his cheek. "It's cool in the tunnels. Wine makers could store barrels, let them age forever. Bring a whole new industry to this shit hole when the war's over."

The jungles of Boi Loi and Ho Bo Woods, located between the Michelin and Filhol Plantations northeast of Cu Chi, were infested with underground networks and booby-trapped trails. Charley hid in thickets too dense to penetrate with human eyes. Sometimes the soldiers would walk down a trail and know Charley was watching; sometimes they'd clear a village and have the sense Charley had been laughing at their backs.

Paez no longer dawdled over the *Stars and Stripes;* he rid himself of Gloria's letters; he eschewed talk that went beyond hello; he smoked pot daily, and his smile became an introspective, self-knowing smirk, a turn of the upper lip.

One day the platoon found a papa *san* on a trail. He'd been shot through the neck and left dead. As they passed by, each of them shook the old man's hand and wished him a good day. When Paez's turn came, he lit a cigarette and stuck it in the dead man's lips, then sat and chatted. He said that he felt certain the papa *san* was Lucky's father.

Belcher asked what had happened to make Paez so weird.

"His girl never showed in Hawaii," Rowe said.

"Kind'a shit happens," Belcher said. "Nothin' to get weird about. Probably found some Jody."

It was a clear morning, dry and tolerable. "A day for picking daisies," Belcher announced as they spread out to enter a village north of Ben Cat, ten huts that didn't show on a map. Sleeper, a big man, a transfer to the squad, looked over, and claiming this was his last ville, said, "I'm so short I have to look up to see my knees."

A handful of women and children and one old toothless *ong* were on hand to greet them, if looking at the ground with cool stares could be called a greeting. The platoon herded them into the open and searched huts. They found no weapons, nothing but some rice stored in baskets, hardly enough to supply a VC squad. This village was destitute. The scout screamed and ranted at the old man, who sat mute. James Bull shrugged, said it was a waste of time. He ordered the platoon out.

Paez's replacement, an FNG named Henderson, walked to the left of Sleeper as they stepped over a hedgerow. There came an unexpected pop. Henderson looked to his side, and seeing the Bouncing Betty hanging in the air like a lost can of green beans, hollered, "Holy shit!" Rowe saw the flash as Sleeper was thrust aside as if hit by a car. Though the blast knocked Rowe down, Sleeper's wide body had saved him from the shrapnel.

A pillar of smoke hung where the mine went off. That, Henderson and Sleeper bleeding on the red clay, and the ringing in the men's ears told the story. Each man inventoried body parts before standing. They got up slowly. Henderson was dead. Sleeper strained to get up but couldn't with just one arm. With his one remaining eye he saw the shredded limb that used to be his left arm. He tried to crawl to it, but that was as futile as trying to stand.

"Someone really messed up," he said and lay on his belly.

Medics zipped Henderson in a body bag and called in a dust off. As he lay on a stretcher watching, Sleeper said, "So short I had to look up to see my knees, and some FNG . . . Ain't it a bitch."

Belcher held his one hand and said, "It's a bitch."

James Bull assembled the platoon. These were his second casualties, and he took it harder than a platoon leader in Vietnam should. Men watched him with narrowed eyes as he shed tears and told them losing a man was like losing one of his own family. He said they weren't alert and that's why soldiers die, that from now on their single mission was to kill ten Charleys for every guy they lost.

Paez asked, "Who's keeping a ledger?"

The grunts closest to Paez nodded in agreement. They'd been hardened by Tet—guys got wounded, buddies died, the war went on. This came down to getting home. Body count meant little if you weren't alive to do the counting, and survival amounted to spitting in the right direction.

Lieutenant Bull wheeled about, turned to Mug Tailor, and said, "Shake the men down for drugs. I know some are using them."

The lieutenant stood at the front as Mug Tailor searched in a haphazard, apologetic manner, overlooking the occasional stash he found while digging his fingers in a man's pack. He'd turn the trooper around, take off the backpack and run his hand around inside. The men could see in his eyes when he found something suspicious, but he didn't report it. He had neither the inclination to roll over on a grenade nor the desire to see his men humiliated.

"Nothin' here, sir!" he'd shout, then whisper in the soldier's ear, "Be cool, be cool."

Paez placed his stash atop his backpack and stood with a vacant expression. As he hovered over the pack, Mug Tailor swallowed and looked up at the heavens. He picked up the baggie and asked, "What's this?"

"Oregano, Sarge," Paez said absolutely deadpan.

Sergeant Tailor grimaced. James Bull threw his shoulders back and charged over. Lieutenant Bull told Tailor to hand over the baggie. After smelling it, he paced back and forth. Paez didn't change expression. The platoon leader stopped and propped his fists on his hips. He told the men to smoke, but no one lit up. He towered over Paez, who gazed about unperturbed.

"Paez, this is marijuana," the lieutenant said.

"Sir, it is? The local said it was oregano."

"Paez, do you think I'm stupid?"

"Sir, it's great with spaghetti. I recommend it."

It was theater. They thrived on the ludicrous and smiled as Paez delivered it on stage, a fact not lost on James Bull.

"And you cook a lot of spaghetti here?" he asked.

"Never enough, sir. Not . . . enough."

The lieutenant said he'd give him a chance to change his story, but Paez didn't crack, even when threatened with a court-martial and being busted to private, even when Mug Tailor said he'd put him on point for the rest of his goddamn tour.

Mug Tailor motioned the lieutenant to a tree, where they conferred out of earshot. Rowe closed his eyes and prayed the moment would resolve itself and Paez would come out of it the same smiling guy he'd met in Cu Chi months before. James Bull walked back, dumped the contents of the baggie on the ground, and crushed it under his boot. "I'm going to overlook this, but I'll be watching," he warned. "Sergeant, get these men harnessed up and ready to go."

That afternoon the platoon came across a hole at the edge of a rubber plantation. They secured the perimeter, and James Bull called Paez over to order him down. The lieutenant must have envisioned refusal, certainly reluctance, but Paez quickly shed his gear and accepted the flashlight and pistol from Tailor. He looked at Rowe, mouthed the name Gloria, and descended.

The platoon waited in the heat, measuring minutes in sweat that beaded on their heads and drenched their fatigues. From time to time the lieutenant would ask Mug Tailor what Paez was doing down there. "Does he think we can hang around being targets forever? Just what the hell does he think he's doing?" Mug Tailor had no answer.

James Bull kept one eye on the hands of his watch and one on the hole and paced back and forth. When twenty minutes had elapsed, he tossed off his helmet, bent over the hole on all fours and called down. "Paez, get your ass up here! Do you hear, Paez? That's a goddamn order!" There came no answer. Belcher smiled sardonically at Rowe, who'd positioned himself near the hole.

James Bull called Mug Tailor over to summon Paez out of the monkey hole. The platoon sergeant came away with the same response. The lieutenant sat on his helmet. He looked at Rowe and said to no one in particular, "This war isn't a joke, and he won't turn it into one."

James Bull waited another hour, shouting red-faced orders down into the hole from time to time, before he summoned Loftin, a slight kid with acne, who didn't talk unless drinking and then wouldn't shut up. Lieutenant Bull told him to go after Paez and get him out of there or someone would face a court-martial.

"Sir, he's got the .45 and the flashlight," Loftin said. "'Sides, if he's comin' out, we'd just butt heads."

"Are you afraid, soldier?"

"Sir, anyone is who isn't a fool or Paez."

Nevertheless, Loftin went down. As Loftin descended, Rowe pictured an ever-narrowing tunnel, one so pinched it pinned Paez's hips so that as the hole got dimmer and dimmer and the batteries drained off, Paez could neither go forward nor with-draw. When twenty minutes later Loftin came up out of another hole beyond the perimeter, he reported following a maze, tun-nels that crisscrossed one another, but no Paez.

"No Paez?" John Bull asked as if he'd not heard.

"No, sir. Nothing but tunnels and a bomb shelter near as I could tell."

"But you couldn't see?"

"No, sir."

Twice more Loftin descended, and twice more came out alone with nothing new to report. The rest of the company proceeded on the operation, leaving the platoon bivouacked on the spot. That evening a chopper brought food in and a flashlight and another .45. After eating, Loftin went down and found two cam-ouflaged openings and another bomb shelter, but no evidence of Paez.

That night, after watch, Rowe lay beside the hole and covered his shoulders with his poncho. The sitting shadow of James Bull hovered near the other side of the opening. He'd not moved since chow. Rowe sent thoughts down into the tunnel until his eyelids fluttered.

Before dawn Rowe awoke and sat up. The lieutenant still sat in the same spot. His anger had faded, and his puffy, heavy-lidded eyes were filled with bafflement. He looked at Rowe and said it had been a long night.

When the others were up and moving, James Bull called a meeting of squad leaders. He asked Belcher and the others what they thought, but no one came up with an explanation. All the while, Rowe sat by the hole, transfixed. Even when it was appar-ent that Paez wasn't coming out, even as James Bull said, "We've stopped the war long enough for this," and commanded the pla-toon to form a column and head out of the plantation, Rowe sat and stared.

James Bull ordered him to his feet. Rowe wanted to rise. His legs simply refused to move. James Bull said he was refusing to follow a lawful command, but said it with compassion. "Come on, son, we don't need trouble, do we?"

Rowe remembered what he'd said in the recruiter's office about wanting to be a killer. He'd said it for the sake of shock. That was long ago. Now he didn't want to shock anyone; he just couldn't move.

Belcher came over and gently hoisted Rowe. He braced him against a shoulder. "Him and Paez, they're buddies," he explained. "Went through Tet together."

James Bull, who by then had recovered some of himself, nodded and said, "Get him up and moving, Sergeant." He left to join the center of the column.

Belcher sought help from another soldier and together they urged Rowe away, Belcher assuring him that Paez had found an opening and was somewhere nearby laughing. "Remember how he joked, always the joker."

Rowe couldn't remember. Just that hole. And Belcher had used the past tense—all the evidence Rowe needed.

In order to shorten his enlistment, Rowe took a three-month extension in Vietnam. It didn't matter. The Army was the same everywhere if you weren't in the boonies. He wore clean fatigues and drank cold beer, stood guard at night and listened to that relentless artillery piece chuck bulletins out to Charley.

He was initially delegated to an officers' club as a waiter, but by accident found an assignment in the Eighteenth Military History Detachment because the lieutenant in charge of keeping records of the Wolfhounds wanted a well-read soldier who could "slip through the smoke screen and write an accurate, readable battle summary." He monitored casualty figures, tracked bulletins and names of MIAS and POWS and KIAS, but was interested in only one, Paez, who remained an MIA. The remainder was boring—filing photographs and composing synopses of dispatches, mostly unnecessary work made to seem important.

Rowe spent those months listening to Lieutenant Horn talk

about going out in the boonies with his own platoon. He envisioned himself a leader, spoke of the glory of combat. Rowe didn't bother to wise him up, no point. Division history was as close as he'd ever come to war. Short and round, he wore glasses that could magnify a blade of grass to the size of a tree, and he talked alternately in clipped, military jargon and blocked-up, semi-academic speech. Rowe liked him. He made no demands of him and seemed to enjoy Rowe's company.

"What was it like, Hobbes?" he asked, as he had many times.

"This time, sir, I'll tell you the truth. It's like having a nightmare as a kid and you wake up and it's still there and you're a part of it, but you don't think you are. You know what's going down and your body acts, but your mind keeps telling you it's a dream. I guess we just distance ourselves from it, even the guys who were dying acted as if they were watching it happen."

"Is that really how it is?"

"No, sir, that's all bullshit. In fact, it's one big non-ending orgasm, a pulsating sensation that swells and shrinks and swells again immediately. Imagine a two-foot hard-on in all that noise and the confusion. The only trouble is it's a wet dream. And that's how it really is."

"Hobbes, you're a philosopher."

"No, sir, just a nothing REMF."

"Don't be hard on yourself. Did I ever tell you about the second battle of the Cynocephalai?"

"Yes, sir."

"Put the Romans in charge of everything. We've been the Romans. Now we're holding on to a dying civilization that never had culture except for jazz and baseball."

"Sir, may I go to the EM club for a beer?"

"Sure, but remember your toxic reaction."

"Yes, sir."

When Lieutenant James Bull's name showed up KIA, awarded the Purple Heart and recommended for a Silver Star, Rowe felt no satisfaction or sorrow. Bull couldn't be held accountable. He was dead, a name, a statistic along with many. Belcher caught an RPG while sitting atop a track near Dau Tieng. Half the platoon was killed or wounded in action. Rowe was lucky. All he had was malaria.

He figured out on his own that he'd contracted the disease. Malaria was what had hit him in Hawaii. Despite identifying the attacks for what they were, he avoided treatment. It was easy to take a day or two away from cataloging photographs and writing one-paragraph battle summaries. It wasn't as if there was any rush to record the history of a war that kept replicating itself.

He kept the seizures to himself, lied and said he was hung over when the fever hit. He informed Lieutenant Horn that he had a brain disorder much like epilepsy, but not, and one of the idiosyncrasies of the condition was the occasional toxic reaction to alcohol. Horn pushed his glasses up and said he understood, that if he'd gone through what Rowe had experienced, he'd turn to booze himself. When asked why he didn't report to sick bay, Rowe answered that the Army would discharge him. Being a graduate of the Citadel, Horn figured that Rowe was simply being honorable. Rowe wondered how he'd feel about honor if he was in the boonies with thirty-five grunts who wanted to burn a village.

Rowe also kept quiet about his symptoms because he'd heard the Army postponed discharges for soldiers who came down with incurable diseases. There was rumor of a secret island for soldiers with incurable VD. The Army kept it like a leper colony, but there only penises rotted off.

Occasionally the muted racket of a distant encounter drifted into camp, a battle at some far-off dot on the province map, sounds that seemed almost benign and left Rowe to wonder if he'd actually experienced something out there. Perhaps he'd just imagined everything, even Paez. War seemed inconceivable, something that happened once upon a time when he was stoned — or was he straight? He felt like a malingerer or quitter, and now and then, a coward.

Once a week he'd hitch a ride on an APC or flag a helicopter flight into Saigon, where he'd ring his mother. If he got in a second call, he'd dial his Uncle Harve in his office or Grady, who was always full of questions, the main one being when Rowe would get tired of playing soldier. Rowe wanted to know about Betty, her marriage and all, half hoping it had failed, but that was one subject he never brought up. There wasn't much time for a lot of chatting, which didn't matter, for there was little to be said. Familiar voices were what Rowe was after, connections with loved ones who didn't go down holes and never come out.

When they'd hang up, he'd feel utterly severed, a reaction just the opposite of what he'd hoped for. It was always the same. Their world had spun smoothly on its usual axis. He'd find himself staring at blank space, projecting himself into the field where he'd watch Paez go down that hole, again and again and again.

When it was Rowe's turn to mount the stairs and climb aboard a freedom bird, he counted the steps and stopped at the door, where a flight attendant welcomed him into the air-conditioned cabin. His seat was just behind the wing on the left side by a window. Attendants came around with their tidy clothes and sure smiles to remind the men to buckle up and put the seat backs in an upright position.

The plane taxied down the runway, gaining speed. There was a last tire skid and the heaviness of the earth slipped away as if a carpet had been yanked out from underneath the wheels. The cabin erupted in cheers. Rowe didn't root, barely heard the racket, in fact. He gazed northward to the quilted countryside, rice paddies and rubber plantations, and beyond in the direction of Boi Loi Woods, which appeared soft and grainy like a picture slightly out of focus.

From that distance the canopy seemed the texture of a cotton bath mat, something soft that God could dry His feet on. Somewhere in that dense, harmless-appearing foliage was one hole, barely big enough to accommodate a small man, and deep inside it Paez, burrowing like a badger, was digging his way to America while Rowe was taking the easy route.

A terrifying sensation, a dark panic, engulfed him. He felt as if in his haste to go, he'd left something behind, something he couldn't remember. Already clock hands were turning inside Rowe's head, ticking off time on the face of a void that soon would be filled with living in the world—perhaps some bourgeois life, some dull dream he would not be able to escape, or if he were lucky, something better. But he felt as he sat watching out the window that someday in the future a phone would ring, a blaring ring, like an alarm, and he would rush to answer it. And on the other end of the line he'd expect to hear the Tunnel Rat's voice . . .

The plane tilted, and the sun's blinding glare shot up from the mirrored surface of a rice paddy. When Rowe again could see clearly, Boi Loi and the Black Virgin Mountain and all of Tay Ninh Province and War Zone C had evaporated on the horizon. He felt a tug on his sleeve.

"What will you have, sir?" the attendant asked.

She must have repeated the question without him hearing. He looked at her as if at an apparition, which she was anyhow. Didn't she know she was an illusion, an image of what they were supposed to believe war was about?

"Do you have Mai Tais?" he asked.

"Sorry, just miniatures."

She held her smile as an outfielder holds a ball barely caught on the fingertips of his glove—hesitant, hopeful. She knew about them. Anything might set them off.

"I'll have a Jack Daniel's," Rowe said. "On ice." Saying it sounded terribly civilized.

Gunning for Ho

I know now I'd expected all along to hear from Bruce, but I'd hoped otherwise. When I left 'Nam, I tried to put it behind me. I never again wanted to see tall grass and vine tangles or low-hanging clouds. I needed open space with distant mountains, a place I understood. I yearned for a strong motorcycle and a long highway. I went home to Nevada, got that bike, found a highway lined with sage and Joshua trees, and started over. I erected solid walls—college degrees, family, teaching career—and made every effort to insulate myself from the past. Yet when some frantic vet killed his family, or when another used the Golden Gate to go airborne for a few seconds before splattering memories and brain pain on a shore-bound wave, I'd think of Bruce.

I picked up the receiver, but before I could speak, he said in an imperious tone, "I told you I'd be in touch, Lum."

The phone went cold in my hand. I'm a guy who wants to know where the keys are and what locks they open. Things fit, books end, holes have bottoms. Once, my worst imaginable fear had been falling into a bottomless shaft, plummeting deeper and deeper into darkness, head swirling, lungs bloated. Then, a guy called twenty-six hours before his death and that quickly changed.

Only Bruce ever called me Lum, and hearing it said with that peculiar arrogant license left me mute and trying to conjure up a face to fit the voice. I remembered him as young man who could dream only one dream at a time. But his face had long since lost shape and, over time, had found form on the pained mug of a homeless man begging change or the resolute expression of a politician campaigning on a war record.

I gathered my wits and said, "Bruce! Jesus, Bruce, it's been a long time."

Undaunted, Bruce said, "What are you doing in a dot on a map called Boulder City?"

"Teaching, raising a family."

"Have you forgotten?"

"Forgotten?"

He said, "Never mind, Lum. Time has come to straighten out things."

"Things?" I asked.

"You know, expose the noble nature of our mission to a world of ingrates and skeptics," he said.

Words had always come from his tongue as if licked off a page of poetry by Kipling, and his pompous tone remained much the same.

"We were the only hope, Lum," he said as if I'd not spoken.

"Hope?"

I recalled the conversation twenty-six years earlier in a Nha Trang, bar conversation that at the time had seemed so much numb-lipped talk from a future Section Eight. I didn't want to discuss the past, and made it clear by changing the subject. I told him my daughters' names, Amy and Sarah, said that they were bright, and my wife worked as a loan officer at a bank in Las Vegas.

He said that was nice and all, then told me to watch television the next day, that the screen would tell the truth. He hung up without a good-bye. For several minutes I stood holding the dead receiver to my chest, thinking.

■

Bruce was the guy who took R&R in Singapore and ended up spending six days in bed with an Australian nurse, the kind of guy who could turn a moment his way or make everyone miserable while he tried. Though he was not charming, he was charmed. Either way, charm only went so far.

I'd seen him around Smoke Bomb Hill, always alone, a cocky kid, a medic, who wore his beret at a radical slant and never seemed to notice anyone else. We finally met one night playing touch football on the damp grass of the parade ground under glaring white stadium lights. It was an amiable push-and-bump game, a bit of fire, no one after blood. Except Bruce.

His energy made him seem somehow bigger than he truly was. He had a tapered trunk and thick legs and was half a head shorter than I was, but he played as if much taller, leaping and snatching the ball with sure hands and perfect timing. He had powerful thighs and keen balance that allowed him to fake, pivot sharply, and still keep his footing. He'd cut on me, gain a step, and take off downfield, and every time he caught a pass, he'd grin and say, "Want it?" He'd toss the ball in my face and race back to the huddle, clapping and leaving me red-faced. He scored his team's four touchdowns on my flat-footed errors. One came when I fell where the grass was slickest. On the way back to the huddle he flipped the ball to me and said, "What a lum!"

We tallied number four on a fly pass to a kid from the Sixth Special Forces, then traded touchdowns. It was five all. First team to six won, and they had the ball.

"Hup, hup," their tailback shouted, took the snap, and back-pedaled. His neck muscles knotting, Bruce pumped his arms up and down and came straight at me. I timed his stride and waited. I wanted the wet grass and a two-step cushion. He wanted the inside route, which I gave him. Thinking, Don't watch his eyes, I turned to run with him. When he planted his inside foot in the wet grass, I banged him with an elbow, not discernibly, but enough that he went down. I stepped under the ball, reversed direction, and raced in for the TD. End of game.

Bruce came up hollering interference.

"You elbowed me!" he shouted.

Ours was a game based on sportsmanship and honor, and I was required to admit the foul. I tossed the football up softly and caught it in one hand. I squared up to look him in the eye, said, "No, I didn't," and flipped the ball in his face.

He demanded the game go on, but the rule was six TDs, no more, no less. Nobody changed the rules. The rest of us shook hands, slipped on our shirts, and started for the club, brushing grass and dirt off our fatigues as we walked. Suddenly he blind-sided me full force, and I went down, Bruce raking my face with fingernails, which seemed an oddly hysterical thing to do. It took six guys to drag him off.

I got orders five weeks later—APO Vietnam—and began pre-mission training. Bruce was in foreign language school learning Spanish for a mission in the Dominican Republic, gravy duty. History, I thought, but a week later, beret still tilted at that cocky slant, he showed at our unit. His face was as open as the horizon as he said, "I went to the Pentagon and found a colonel in a closet, a desk in a six-by-six room. He cut me orders on the spot. We'll be going to 'Nam together." He offered a handshake and said, "No hard feelings. I'm not one to enjoy losing. Hate it, in fact." The scratches he'd put on me hadn't yet healed. Less than overjoyed, I reluctantly took his hand.

* * *

Bruce's eyes were blue, and behind them—if you looked closely—was a solitary and turbulent world. He was a marvel of intensity, his nimble fingers field-stripping all manner of weapons on the first try, as if he'd blueprinted each one. If he held a grudge, it never showed in how he treated me. He'd see me fumbling to get a trigger housing out and come to my aid. Making it look simple, he would disassemble the piece, wink at me, and say, "Got it now, Lum?" When I did it right, he'd pat my shoulder to encourage me.

When he did talk, Bruce spoke about war and Vietnam, offering minute details about Dien Bien Phu and the French collapse, the complexity and implications of the British victory in Malaya, and the ill-fated concept of strategic hamlets in 'Nam. I listened but didn't care. How could knowing the history of a war zone keep me alive?

Over the weeks we trained together, I pried bits of private history from him. Though we were quite different, he insisted we weren't, and no amount of arguing could persuade him against it. I came from the Southwest, the second son of a long-suffering mother and a stubborn father who'd given up farming hardpan in New Mexico to lower bombs underground by crane at the nuclear test site. Bruce, on the other hand, came from privilege, from an old New England family with money and clout. He'd graduated Andover and later attended Norwich University for a year. He claimed, without elaboration, that there had been a "spat."

"Sometimes, Lum, I find it difficult to negotiate with people. But you, I like."

For whatever reason, be it imagining me lucky or because of my kind of steady pluck, he adopted me. Though never cozy with the idea, I went along with it.

One night at Caruso's in Fayetteville, we sat in a booth and nursed beers. I'd put in four quarters and punched E-6 twelve times. I was into beer and sad songs, especially "The Dock of the Bay." In the din of loud conversation and barmaids taking orders from drunks, it was hard to even hear a song. A big, hard-knuckled paratrooper from the Eighty-second was seated with three buddies in the next booth. When my song came on the fourth time, he bellyached about people being rude and having no taste in music. Bruce stared straight at him until the guy had to say something.

"What's your problem?" the paratrooper asked.

Undaunted, Bruce said, "My friend here just lost a wife. This was her favorite song. That is my problem."

The paratrooper looked down at the floor, apologized, and then ordered us a pitcher of beer.

Bruce raised his mug. "Lum," he said, as he'd taken to calling me, "it's now my favorite song, next to the Largo from the *New World Symphony*. Bet you like Georges Braque, dissected guitars, and violins in ochre and black and brown." That was true, and I liked Dvořák as well. But how could he know?

Taking the Vomit Comet back to the fort, we found a seat in the back of the bus, where it was unlikely for a soldier to throw up on us, as sometimes happened. Bruce took the aisle seat and stretched out for the ride. As we slowed at the entrance, a para-trooper two seats up turned to say something to his buddy. He picked that moment to get sick, all over the aisle. Bruce looked down at his shoes, which had been splattered, then at mine, which were untouched.

"You're lucky. You know that, don't you, Lum? A very lucky sort," he said.

Other than on weekends, Bruce was all business. He pushed him-self in drills and on tests, jogged alone in the muggy autumn heat of the orange-skied evenings. I conditioned myself at the EM club on pretzels, draft beer, and moody songs, a pace more suited to me. At the end of the training cycle, he'd scored highest on every test. Figuring Vietnam was the true final exam, I did well enough to pass.

A week before shipping out, we were granted leave. I wanted a week in Myrtle Beach, hoping to encounter some lonely Southern belle and live a fantasy or two. If not, a walk on the boardwalk and a splash in the Atlantic seemed just fine. Bruce made other plans and convinced me to hitchhike with him to D.C., where he'd met three coeds from Georgetown University.

They put us up in their apartment. He told me to play along with their gig. "Lum," he said, "these girls are dedicated to undermining the war, radicals. Get the drift?" I shook my head. He told me they'd do *anything* to get us to desert. Celeste, Lorraine, and Sheila spent the week grounding us in Marxist dogma as we smoked dope, drank beer, and mingled with them on a pile of throw pillows strewn about an otherwise empty room. At week's end they seemed disappointed that we'd decided not to take the back door into Canada. They asked us to promise not to kill any Viet Cong, which we did so as not to shatter their illusions.

We hitched a ride to Bragg in the back of a pickup with a blue plastic camper shell. Bruce uncapped a pint of tequila and said, "To kicking ass." I downed a jolt, said, "To surviving," and handed him the bottle. He capped it, and as he slipped it in his pocket, said he hoped we'd be sent to the same camp, figuring that as I was demo man and he was a medic, there might be chance of it happening. I hadn't given the idea a first thought, and realized I didn't want to give it a second.

In country, Bruce was assigned to Luc Lon Duc Biet Headquarters in Dong Ba Tinh, where nothing happened, and I went to Tra Bong. Four months later on an in-country R&R, I was seated in a club near the beach in Nha Trang. The night was sultry but not unpleasant, mosquitoes buzzing as we drank and listened to the high-pitched hustle of bar girls. A voice behind me said, "I knew we'd cross paths."

Without asking, he took a chair opposite me and leaned across the table. "Lum," he said, "I've been here four months. Four stinking months, had the clap five times, and smoked some shit that would stew a moose, but I've not put a sight on a single Cong. I volunteered to kill Charley and this is a spiritless life I'm leading."

He ordered five shots of tequila. He lined the jiggers up on the table and set his watch in front of him to time himself as he gulped them down at ten-minute intervals. Between swallows, he asked about Tra Bong and listened intently as I described it. After the last shot vanished, he squinted and aimed a forefinger at my nose. "It'll do," he said.

At the next table where five Special Forces sergeants sat drinking, a boom-boom girl hiked up her skirt and crawled under the table. Bruce shook his head as her torso disappeared. "Zipper roulette," he said. He told me we were too worried about nightclubs and nooky. To be effective we had to crawl into the jungle and live off snakes and insects. He stood up unsteadily and rocked back and forth. In an effort to change the subject, I asked if he liked Green Bay in the NFL Championship.

"Football, Lum," he said loudly. "You think I've forgotten?"

Others were watching. I said he should sit.

"Sit, hell," he yelled and said he was tired of sitting and watching. He was a player, by God, and would go to Westmoreland himself to get off the bench.

One of the sergeants told me I should take my buddy back to the base. When Bruce finally passed out, I propped him on my shoulder and carried him to the transient billets at the Operational Base. There I dumped him on the first empty bunk. He came to and said the only way was to crawl into the jungle.

I said, "Let's just zap Uncle Ho, then we can all go home."

He came out of his fog. Closed one eye and stared as if seeing me for the first time. "Right," he said. He dozed off and began snoring immediately.

Three weeks later, fate and a Huey brought Bruce to Tra Bong. He hopped down into a plume of violet smoke and grinned as the chopper ascended. He gazed up the pipe of long emerald valley, at the mountains and moss-covered cliffs. When all was silent except for the distant thrumming of the helicopter engine, he tightened his fist on his M-16 and said, "Lum, this is more like it."

Bruce didn't drink a drop of alcohol and spurned all but the minimal duties of a medic. As the rest of us played pinochle, he and the team captain, a West Pointer, talked history and military strategy, especially the Civil War. The captain, a Virginian, spoke from the perspective of the South and Bruce from that of the North. Nothing less than Sherman's strategy, Bruce claimed, was acceptable in war. He endeared himself to the captain, who soon allowed him to advise the Recon Platoon, a unit made up of Coho tribesmen, mountain people who came from the highland forests.

Bruce bribed his flat-faced wards with cigarettes and candy, ate with them, learned their lingo and Vietnamese as well. I taught him demolitions, and in no time he could crimp a blasting cap by feel and wire any model detonator with his clever fingers. He volunteered for night ambushes, but the more often he went out, the less pleased he seemed.

Before leaving for R&R, he pulled me aside and said, "This isn't what I came here for. It won't do at all. Remember what you said in Nha Trang." It wasn't a question.

I didn't remember saying anything.

When he returned, he picked up where he'd left off. After two successful ambushes, he convinced the captain to send the platoon out in search of North Vietnamese and order in "a fury from the heavens on them." The captain admired tenacity and would have honored any request Bruce put to him. Bruce asked one additional thing—that I, too, go on the patrol. I mentioned that it wasn't my turn on the roster. No one seemed to hear or care.

We left two hours before daybreak, moving west by northwest. The Coho didn't use trails or skirt mountains. As we humped up and down the steep slopes, we saw sign after sign of Charley—

tunnels and bunkers—and we passed spot after spot ideal for an ambush. Bruce kept his own counsel. I didn't like the drift of things, but that didn't amount to anything much, not deep in the forest where we were utterly dependent upon one another.

The second day I suspected he had given false coordinates over the radio, but I didn't say anything, just watched.

The third day we were near Laos. As we paused on a rocky promontory overlooking a series of lesser peaks, I grabbed his sleeve and asked what was up. He calmly pried my fingers off his biceps and pushed my hand away. He nodded and looked about.

"Relax, Lum," he said. "We're about to end this. Time has come. I'm going all the way to Hanoi to put a .223 right between Uncle Ho's Marxist eyes, and you're going to cover my ass."

Looking down into his eyes, I realized that I'd never once heard Bruce laugh, just an occasional throaty aping of it. He wasn't the kind to crack a joke. "It's a touch crazy, Bruce," I said.

"A stupendous observation, Lum. The little fucker's got our whole army manacled. I intend to change that." He dragged a forefinger slowly across his throat.

We stood looking at one another, running the idea over in our minds as if calculating pass patterns. It was hypothetical intrigue, the kind of idea that fell out like loose change on the bar, the kind you'd hear or express after four or five shots of tequila at a nightclub in Nha Trang. Like screwing Ursula Andress, it was a great idea with no chance of success.

"Hanoi's a long way off," I said, stepping to my right, thinking I might be able to get to the radio. "How do you figure to get there?"

With a forefinger, he motioned to the Montagnard and said, "A trail named Ho Chi Minh should put us right on his doorstep. If the little murderers can use it to come south, we can use it to go north."

I saw in his blue eyes that he was serious. So much for puffed-up fantasy. "We'll never make it," I said.

"Hannibal crossed the Alps against all odds."

"I'm not Hannibal and neither are you," I said.

"No, but I might have been." He looked at the distant peaks, his eyes flashing as he smiled to himself.

Half the Ba Mui Ba beer in South Vietnam wouldn't make the idea float. As I groped for some way to convince him it wouldn't work, I moved again slightly. "We'd be deserting."

"Killing the enemy isn't desertion. After it's over, we'll share a few shots and a lot of memories."

I asked where he ever got such a crazy idea.

"You."

"Me?"

I saw the Montagnards pressing in. He called over the one who carried our PRC-25.

"I see you're a doubting Thomas, Lum," he said as he lifted the radio from the Coho's back. He held it overhead, momentarily looking in my direction, then he sent it tumbling down a sheer cliff, where it landed on a rocky bed three hundred feet below. He looked back at me and said, "Now, let's go get that rice-thieving little dictator."

As we lay in ambush that night, I thought of crawling away but didn't. Sounds of bombs dropped by B-52s two mountain ranges to the west kept me awake. I felt Bruce watching me in the dark. I slept fitfully for an hour or two. The next morning and throughout the day as we trudged through the forest, we heard the drone of L-10 Bird Dogs in the air above the jungle canopy. By nightfall the search planes were gone and the sky was silent and invisible to us. In the morning he patted my shoulder and said, "Rules just aren't for guys like us."

Everything in the jungle that moved had fangs, and everything that didn't had thorns. We endured insufferable heat during the day and shivered at night. In four days our food was gone. Bruce had been wise in choosing the Coho. They kept us alive in the jungle, feeding us termite grubs and roots, all manner of leaf and the occasional snake, diced and raw. Bruce said I was thinking too narrowly. He tried to lift my spirits, insisting I would be better off seeing the big picture.

Two weeks after we had left camp, a mass of scratches and insect bites, we first glimpsed the trail that led north. It was a hive of human activity, a crude road of mud and cord wood, busy with supply trucks and elephants and soldiers marching on sandals made of old tires, a few riding bicycles, all going south in a singularly fierce display of energy and purpose. They passed within yards of us as we waited in the bush. I glanced at Bruce and saw all I needed to see. He wasn't afraid.

Once we awoke beside a trail where, unbeknownst to us, a detachment of North Vietnamese had quartered for the night. Bruce drew a bead on an officer who looked to be the commander. "Think he realizes he's as good as dead?" Bruce whispered—but didn't pull the trigger. He was after bigger stuff.

Sometime in the third week Bruce had abandoned the idea of using Uncle Ho's highway to the north. We'd long since passed outside the boundaries of our maps. Each day the same patterns unfolded, marching in heat up and down mountains buried under a rain-forest canopy, slivers of sunshine the only light, sweat, exhaustion, thorns that shredded leather and fatigues. Leeches fed off us, bayonet leaves stabbed us, knife-edged grass cut us, rocks dug into the soles of our boots. Each night we collapsed on the hard ground, and as insects crawled over our numb bodies, we slept fitfully. We had entered the jungle as Bruce had said we must. Doing it had changed nothing, and we were still hundreds of miles away from Uncle Ho's citadel.

That third week the Montagnard wearied of the quest and even of Bruce. Politics meant nothing to them, and loyalty, even the best kind, goes only so far. Two came down with malaria. Bruce ordered a squad to take them back. But no one could be sure where *back* was, because by then we didn't know where we were. One of their rank said we should all go back. Refusing to take another step, they squatted down and stared off in the distance.

Instead of being discouraged, Bruce was elated to confront a mutiny. He seemed like a man beckoned by an angel or a demon. Such men know how to inspire. He pointed first to the south, then the north, waved his arms and walked about hollering. Without knowing their language, I deduced what Bruce said as he harangued them. He called them quitters, warning that they'd be shot for desertion if he didn't return with them. He petitioned their manhood, said the outcome of the war depended on the mission. He let them discuss it. They gathered in a circle and debated the situation calmly. A few minutes later a representative approached Bruce and nodded.

The trek continued. Although I kept moving, I was determined to get away. My options were limited to staying with him and getting killed on some impossible scheme or taking off into a Viet Cong–infested jungle on my own without map or compass. Out of two not great choices, the first was worse. I had to keep watch and bide my time. Bruce was human, and humans tire and make mistakes. I would wait for that mistake; if he didn't make one, I'd have to kill him.

One morning about a week later we stumbled upon a small unit of NVA regulars sleeping by a pagoda on a slope overlooking a mist-filled valley. We killed nine and captured two. They had rice balls and tins of fish in oil. We sat in the shade, ate the dead men's food, and watched the two prisoners, who were quite young and quite scared. In them, I saw a glimmer of hope. The Geneva Convention demanded that we care for them. I said we'd have to take them back. Bruce shot them each in the head, turned to me, and said, "You understand these are novel circumstances, Lum."

I'd had it with plum dreams. That afternoon as we crossed a stream in the dense forest, I eased back to let the Montagnard pass one at a time. I saw my chance. Exhausted, Bruce was too tired to notice as I slipped away. And so were the Montagnard. I waited until they were safely out of earshot and plunged downhill, half running, half tumbling and sliding. The dense undergrowth muffled my sounds. I came to a combe darkened by the thick canopy of tree boughs. Everything was so shaded that leaves seemed gray instead of green. I stopped here and listened for them. Certainly they would come. I counted on that, and soon they did. They were tired and so made more noise than normal. One slipped and the butt of a carbine struck a rock. I crawled into the underbrush and hid in a vine tangle at the base of a tree as they combed the brush looking for me.

Very soon I noticed that I was sharing the tangle with a rather large red-eyed boa constrictor that hung on a low limb. I'd watched this scene once or twice in Tarzan movies and had no wish to duplicate the life-and-death struggle with a fifteen-foot snake, nor did I want to shoot it. But then again, I knew diced snake tasted better than beetles and grubs.

At one point Bruce stood a few yards away, talking with his troops. They scoured about for me for an hour or so. The snake, apparently deciding I was too much of a mouthful, left when they did. Even as I heard them trudge off, heading north, I remained hidden in the tangle throughout the night, just in case. The next morning I found a stream and followed it southeast.

After weaving through a maze of enemy encampments, two weeks later I approached Khe Sanh. My skin, dark as the mud surrounding the camp, was blotched and bleeding. My boots were shredded, my fatigues threadbare and ripped. Having survived mostly on grubs, I was terribly emaciated and barely strong enough to speak. Raising my M-16 overhead, I rose up from behind a bush, and a Marine standing guard shot me.

A single round passed through my side without nicking bone, artery, or vital organ. I was lucky, but not lucky enough to go home. Officers from Nha Trang debriefed me in the hospital. I told them Bruce and I had lost the radio and maps, said that we'd wandered about lost for weeks, until we'd gotten separated cross-ing a stream. I didn't mention his plan or the dead prisoners. As far as I knew, he was alive, but I never expected to see him again. I was rewarded with a job at Group Headquarters. A month later, stitched and mending, I was flown from Okinawa to Vietnam. Bruce was listed as Missing in Action.

Occasionally, in the weeks to follow, as I sat drinking a brew or two, I'd find myself anticipating news that Ho Chi Minh had been killed. If there was a way, if Bruce's charmed life held up . . . Instead the news that finally came gave me reason to worry. His soldiers had abandoned him and had scattered south and east, following river routes. They added nothing to my story, except to confirm that Bruce was MIA. That was when I realized they had no idea what Bruce had been up to.

The news I'd most feared arrived two months later. At my desk one afternoon at Group Headquarters, I was thumbing through a Psy-Ops document when Lieutenant Savage threw a memo down and said, "Stoner's been found." After having been captured in Laos by the North Vietnamese, he'd been toted about in a bamboo cage and displayed in villages. A company from the 101st Airborne had liberated him.

After spending two weeks being treated in a field hospital, he was flown to Group Headquarters. A major and a lieutenant colonel from G-2 sat across the table from him. Lieutenant Savage and I sat beside the senior officers. Dark and shriveled as jerky, Bruce sat looking from face to face. His left hand was mangled. After he explained his wild plan — "the mission," as he called it — the major wanted to know where he ever got such a notion.

Bruce looked at me. "Lum, tell them."

I looked away and shrugged. After a few seconds he realized I wasn't going to speak. He nodded, and without blinking, claimed he'd been ordered by the Pentagon and that the White House had approved it. He faced the major and calmly said, "Assassination is the politics of Vietnam, sir."

"Why," the colonel asked, "didn't we hear of this?"

Bruce didn't answer, just said, "They ran bamboo up my penis, sir. Broke my fingers." He held up the two gnarled digits. "I gave name, rank, and serial number. They have no idea what I was up to. We could start all over." He looked at me again and fell silent.

Afterward the colonel pulled me aside and told me, as Bruce was my friend, to baby-sit him until they could ship him stateside for evaluation. We went to a nightclub near the beach, where we drank tequila shooters with Ba Mui Ba backs. He talked about the torture, but said worse was the pain of no one believing it could be done.

"You believe, don't you?" he asked.

I didn't, but I nodded and downed a shot of tequila.

When I said it was time to go, he grabbed my forearm with his gnarled left hand and squeezed. Despite his weakened state, there was enormous strength in his fingers. "Lum," he said, "there's no hard feelings. It was your idea, but it was my job to do. I'm sorry I got you involved." He stood and shook my hand. "You'll hear from me."

■

Bruce's phone call left me preoccupied to the exclusion of most everything else. I waited out the rest of the day and the night, his phone call in the forefront of my thoughts. The more I remembered details about those months spent with him, the deeper my concern ran. My wife asked several times what was on my mind. I pretended I had a headache, even took an ice pack to bed with me to convince her. The past crowded my mind — conversations with Bruce, a moment sharing raw bird eggs beside a mountain stream. No matter how I juggled memories, I came back to the night I had bumped into Bruce in Nha Trang when his drunken eyes opened in a moment of awareness.

I gave my students in-class writing assignments and spent the school day pulling out old forms that needed attention, blowing dust from folders, staring out the window. I jumped at the sound of the phone and the school bell. A sense of reckoning pervaded every small act that day, like knowing there was a wasp in my pocket and knowing also that I must reach in for change.

Our home, one of two hundred built when Hoover Dam was under construction, is a modest one-story house with a wood floor. My private space is a seven-by-nine room. That evening, as Amy watched Sarah imitate a giraffe with a sore throat, I unplugged the portable TV and carried it into my makeshift den, shut the door, and pushed some books aside to make room for the set.

I flipped on the TV and settled into my cushioned chair in time to catch the end of a feature on teenage AIDS, followed by a short commercial for a stockbrokerage firm. After the ad, the anchorman spoke eagerly of a drama unfolding on the grounds at the Pentagon, where a deranged veteran had somehow sneaked past security and was engaged in a standoff with authorities. Then a woman clutching a microphone described in rapid-fire speech that talks were stalemated between police and a disgruntled veteran who refused to surrender.

A camera panned the scene. Bruce, now a chubby-faced forty-eight year old, wearing a beret and a vest of plastic explosives, stood near the entrance to the Pentagon. He looked at the camera with an elfin grin. I pressed the selector. His face flashed on every channel that covered the live news. Another newswoman, updating facts, explained that the unidentified ex-soldier had demanded that information of a clandestine mission be made public, but to what end he wouldn't say.

Coverage shifted to a Pentagon spokesman, a tall, dry-faced Army colonel with a genteel Southern accent. He looked into the cameras as he identified Bruce by name. He said Bruce had served as a Green Beret and received a discharge for medical reasons. Under questioning, he said he wasn't at liberty to elaborate, but there had been no clandestine mission. One reporter asked how Bruce had managed to breach Pentagon security.

"We trained him, didn't we?"

Again the scene shifted. Following a short televised introduction, a presidential aide spoke. "The president's close to this, and his concern is deep. No one has worked harder to indemnify veterans for their gallant service to this nation. He wants old wounds healed, but, as a citizen, is obligated to view this as a police matter and cannot comment further. Questions?"

Bruce stood near the steps of the Pentagon, in his closed right hand a pressure-release detonator. As thirty D.C. SWAT cops kept aim, a negotiator standing behind a mobile barricade spoke through a bullhorn, asking what exactly it was he wanted. Bruce stared into the cameras. Calm and lucid as a diplomat at a state dinner, he said, "Lum knows." Then he lifted his lame hand as if to wave and with his good one released the detonator.

The odd thing about an explosion caught on a microphone is the distortion of sound. It's physics. Shock waves from the instantaneous expansion of gases override the device's capacity to capture sound just as an eardrum plugs up under similar circumstances. The sudden swelling of a flash and the tremor of the camera and the smoke that mutated gradually into a shapely column of dark soot attested to the explosion. The broadcast shifted to the studio and the stunned face of the anchorman, whose silent likeness faded to a Toyota 4-Runner commercial. Only theory was what remained of Bruce, slapdash chatter of hypothesizing reporters.

I had somehow knocked books onto the floor, and as I bent over, Amy tapped at the door and asked if I was okay, said she'd heard something fall, but Bruce now was seated across from me, the glaze gone from his eyes. It still was my room, but he was on a cot in the dark billets as he gazed up at me. I heard only the tapping at the door and the internal hum of the house. Crouched on my hands and knees, I felt the hardwood of the floor. I opened my mouth to speak, but had no air in my lungs to form sound, not even enough to protest. I was at a loss to know how I'd come to be there, but I was, on the floor, dazed, crawling like a baby, or a supplicant, or a mourner.

Afterword

With more than seven hundred novels and short story collections published about Americans fighting in the Vietnam War, a reader is tempted to ask, "What more could there be to say?" This book provides a resounding answer: "Lots."

Lee Barnes fits well into, yet also transcends, one of the two major categories of Vietnam War authors—the men and women who experienced the war, then wrote fiction about it. Many of these writers were on-the-scene correspondents who turned their reporting experiences into often thinly disguised fictional works. Along with many others, Pamela Sanders, Smith Hempstone, David Halberstam, the Kalbs (Bernard and Marvin), and Robin Moore were in-country reporters whose subsequent novels received attention and praise. More predominant, however, is the larger number of writers who served, usually as young enlisted men in the armed forces, then returned home immediately to finish college (usually on the GI Bill) and then attend graduate school, where many of them received M.A.'s and M.F.A.'s in creative writing.

Lee Barnes fits into the latter category, along with Tim O'Brien, Larry Heinemann, James Crumley, and poets Yusef Komunyakaa and W. D. Ehrhart, all of whom have transformed their wartime experiences into significant and acclaimed works of fiction and poetry. Where Barnes differs from the others, however, is that his formal literary avocation arrived long after his combat experiences. After his Vietnam service in 1966, he spent many years as a policeman, then, he says, "tinkered with writing." Only in 1985 did he return to college for his B.A., where he published a novella, *The Mind Is Its Own Place,* before starting his studies for the M.F.A. Not until 1993 did he begin, in his words, "to reexamine Vietnam." The result of his examination is *Gunning for Ho,* this collection of six moving short stories and the remarkable novella "Tunnel Rat."

Perhaps because of his emotional maturity, perhaps because of the distanced perspective he has on his subject matter, Barnes's fiction is quite different from that of other Vietnam War veteran writers who began publishing in the mid- to late sixties. For many years, the typical story or novel has been realistic, gritty, and usually highly critical not only of the American presence in Vietnam and the way the war was being conducted but also of the effects of the war on the soldiers, sailors, and airmen, as well as on Americans at home. Usually based on the writer's own tour of duty, the fiction of the past thirty years has shown well-meaning young men inducted, trained, sent off to kill a shadowy enemy that usually proved unstoppable, and then, physically or at least emotionally wounded, returning home to a country that could not possibly understand what they had just been through. As recently as 1995, Joe Haldeman's excellent novel *1968* (set in the same year as Barnes's novella) follows this general pattern.

Perhaps also because he is now close to the age his parents were when *he* served in Vietnam, Barnes is able, in two of the stories in this collection, "The Cat in the Cage" and "A Return," to look at what might have been as well as what was. Both stories feature fathers trying to come to grips with the deaths of their sons, one by traveling to Vietnam to find the truth about the rumors of his son having been displayed in a Viet Cong cage as a prisoner of war, the other by accepting delivery of his son's remains almost two decades after he was declared missing in action. Another story, "Plateau Lands," has a conflict that is superficially similar to that of Tim O'Brien's *In the Lake of the Woods* (the main character's friend is a Vietnam veteran with a secret who is running for Congress), but Barnes shows his concern not with politics and possibility but with family, as his main character wrestles with what and how to tell his wife about the war.

Barnes also shows a remarkable sense of humor, at once fanciful, then quite black. "A Lovely Day in the A Shau Valley" is both hilarious and very sad, as the North Vietnamese and the Americans first play an exhausting baseball game, then try to blow each other away. In "Stonehands and the Tigress," the meaning of myth predominates as one soldier attempts to give a tiger cub back to its mother, then joins the forces of nature. And in the title story, "Gunning for Ho," what seems madly incongruous becomes shatteringly symbolic as a veteran faces the TV cameras in front of the Pentagon.

In each of these stories, written in different styles and from differing points of view, what predominates is believability, even in those scenes that seem logically implausible. The characters talk to each other, not to the reader, and the language they use, whether pidgin English, Southern dialect, street jargon, or even highly educated literary speech, reveals who they are in a most convincing way.

In general, Barnes's fiction seems to be less about the war itself than about the people who fight in and are affected by it. What characterizes Barnes's vision is, I think, an acceptance of the Vietnam War as irreversible fact and a willingness to use the war as a vehicle for exploring even larger human issues. Not that he ignores the actuality of combat—there are some shattering and grisly scenes—but these stories are not what one has come to see as "usual" war stories.

It is in "Tunnel Rat" that Barnes combines all of his techniques and themes. This novella is on the one hand one of the most realistic depictions yet written about young men and women of the sixties at home and at war, but on the other hand it is a near epic study of relationships and responsibility. All the sights, sounds, smells, and feeling of combat are here, and the dialogue and descriptions are extraordinary. And yes, the novella ends with a great sense of loss, but somehow, despite everything, the reader feels a deep sense of gratitude for having been able to come to know this very special group of people. The scene of the young Vietnamese girls in white *áo dàis* riding their bicycles through the scene of a recent battle is hauntingly memorable and—as is so much of Barnes's fiction—the way it so often really was.

Rather than as an indictment of the Vietnam War, as are so many of the other works of fiction on the subject, *Gunning for Ho* should be read as an inspired testament to those elements of the human spirit that will always, one has to believe, prevail.

John Clark Pratt
Vietnam, Laos, Thailand 1969–70